Pra

"I shuddered as I read eac
novel. Slavenka Drakulić fc a
Bosnian woman made preg a
Serbian prison camp. Every chapter resonates r-
ror and—remarkably, even—hope."

—Iris Chang, bestselling author of *The Rape of Nanking*

"The story of S. is not factual; it is fiction. Nonetheless it is very, very true. Devastatingly true. And *S.* may very well be one of the strongest books about war you will ever read. . . . No doubt empowered by her research, Drakulić has crafted a novel that allows her to get fully into the mind of a woman who has been subjected to the unspeakable. Yet there are no traces of melodrama, cheap shots or political discourses. The writing is taut, precise and masterful. Drakulić brings the full horror of ethnic cleansing to life in a vivid, idiosyncratic way that will haunt the corners of your mind long after the book's final page."

—*The Philadelphia Inquirer*

"Slavenka Drakulić is a courageous and passionate writer from that vanished country, Yugoslavia—a voice to be trusted in an echo chamber of lies. With this book she takes us down into the very heart of the Balkan darkness and then slowly back up to the light. It is fiction with the terrible authority of truth."

—Michael Ignatieff, author of *Isaiah Berlin: A Life*

"Slavenka Drakulić has given the world a gift, digging into the twisted reality of the war that splintered the former Yugoslavia and emerging with *S.*, a searing story about a woman held in a Bosnian concentration camp. It is a haunting, difficult novel that is also somehow redemptive. In the past, Drakulić has demonstrated in essays such as *Café Europa: Life After Communism* an inspired knack for unlikely but telling details. She also has a restlessness and moral imagination that give her work nuance and power and flavor. . . . But never has she combined her approach and her subject matter into anything like the cataclysmic power of this new novel. . . . The book never drags and no page stands out as less gripping than the next."

—*San Francisco Chronicle*

"Slavenka Drakulić has courageously provided some of the most searing commentary on the war that swept her homeland and the whole Balkan region. But to understand its true nature and the mindset of those who pursued the war, one has to know what they did to the women of Bosnia. Beyond painful, beyond brutal, it was almost impossible to comprehend. Once again, Slavenka Drakulić forces us to understand."

—Christiane Amanpour, Chief International Correspondent, CNN

"Drakulić's graphic account of S.'s emotionally wrought experiences puts a human face on harrowing headlines. . . . You might not want to read it at night. Despite its brevity, it is grim and horrific."

—*The Seattle Times*

"In recounting one woman's journey through the dark stations of ethnic conflict, Slavenka Drakulić makes us see what we have perhaps preferred not to confront: the awful depredations of war in the deep regions of body and psyche. If you would understand a central contemporary event in its full, human dimensions, read this spare, unsparing and very moving novel."

—Eva Hoffman, author of *Lost in Translation* and *Exit into History*

"An eloquent scream from the recent past . . . As testimony, *S.* is horrifying and unsentimental. As a novel, this testimony speaks with enormous moral authority. With this amazing and important novel, Drakulić puts a human face on the abstractions of wartime atrocities and ethnic cleansing. It is not easy to look at this face, but it is necessary. *S.* is simultaneously a record of the evil of which people are capable and an investigation into the redemptive power of forgiveness."

—*St. Petersburg Times*

PENGUIN BOOKS

S.

Slavenka Drakulić was born in Croatia in 1949. She is the author of several books of non-fiction, including *Deadly Sins of Feminism; How We Survived Communism and Even Laughed; The Balkan Express: Fragments From the Other Side of War*; and, most recently, *Café Europa: Life After Communism*. She is also the author of three previous novels: *Holograms of Fear*, which was a best-seller in Yugoslavia and was shortlisted for the Best Foreign Book Award by *The Independent* (UK); *Marble Skin*; and *The Taste of a Man*. Drakulić's prose has been compared to that of Marguerite Duras, Samuel Beckett, and Albert Camus. Her books have been published in thirteen countries and translated into twelve languages.

Drakulić is a freelance journalist and novelist who contributes to *The New York Times, The Nation, The New Republic, Frankfurter Alggemeine Zeitung* (Germany), *Dagens Nyheter* (Sweden), and *La Stampa* (Italy), among other international newspapers and magazines. She divides her time between Sweden and Croatia.

S.

A NOVEL ABOUT THE BALKANS

SLAVENKA DRAKULIĆ

TRANSLATED BY
MARKO IVIĆ

PENGUIN BOOKS

PENGUIN BOOKS
Published by the Penguin Group
Penguin Putnam Inc., 375 Hudson Street,
New York, New York 10014, U.S.A.
Penguin Books Ltd, 27 Wrights Lane, London W8 5TZ, England
Penguin Books Australia Ltd, Ringwood, Victoria, Australia
Penguin Books Canada Ltd, 10 Alcorn Avenue,
Toronto, Ontario, Canada M4V 3B2
Penguin Books (N.Z.) Ltd, 182–190 Wairau Road,
Auckland 10, New Zealand

Penguin Books Ltd, Registered Offices:
Harmondsworth, Middlesex, England

First published in Great Britain as *As If I Am Not There* by
Little, Brown and Company (UK) 1999
First published in the United States of America by Viking Penguin,
a member of Penguin Putnam Inc. 2000
Published by Penguin Books 2001

1 3 5 7 9 10 8 6 4 2

Originally published in German as *Als gabe es mich nicht* by Aufbau Verlag GmbH,
Berlin. Published in Croatian under the title
Kao da me nema by Feral Tribune, Split, Croatia.

PUBLISHER'S NOTE
This is a work of fiction. Names, characters, places, and incidents
either are the product of the author's imagination or are used fictitiously,
and any resemblance to actual persons, living or dead, business
establishments events, or locales is entirely coincidental.

THE LIBRARY OF CONGRESS HAS CATALOGUED
THE VIKING HARDCOVER EDITION AS FOLLOWS:
Drakulić, Slavenka, 1949–
[Kao da me nema. English]
S.: novel about the Balkans/Slavenka Drakulić; translated by Marko Ivic.
p. cm.
Running title: As if I am not there.
Translated from Serbo-Croatian (roman)
ISBN 0-670-89097-9 (hc.)
ISBN 0 14 02.9844 4 (pck.)
1. Yugoslav War, 1991–1995—Bosnia and Hercegovina—Fiction.
2. Bosnia and Hercegovina—History—1992–Fiction. 3. Women—Fiction.
4. Refugees—Fiction. 5. Rape—Fiction. I. Title: As if I am not there.
II. Ivic, Marko.
PG1619.14.34.R3A K3613 2000
891.8'2354—dc21 99–054481

Printed in the United States of America
Set in Berling • Designed by Lorelle Graffeo

It is an intense pleasure, physical, inexpressible, to be at home, among friendly people and to have so many things to recount: but I cannot help noticing that my listeners do not follow me. In fact, they are completely indifferent: they speak confusedly of other things among themselves, as if I was not there. My sister looks at me, gets up and goes away without a word.

PRIMO LEVI, *If This is a Man*

And quite unconsciously, perhaps precisely because of the exaggerated sense of fear, I felt at times as if this was not me at all, as if it was happening to somebody else, and everything I had seen was actually part of some other, unreal world.

EVA GRLIĆ, *Memoirs*

A human being survives by his ability to forget.

VARLAM SHALAMOV, *Kolyma Tales*

Karolinska Hospital, Stockholm

27 MARCH 1993

The child is lying naked in his cot. He is stretched out on a sheet, perfectly still, his arms and legs splayed, like someone surrendering.

S. sees the little fingers with their tiny real-life nails. The child's head is turned to the side. He is asleep and in his slumber he sucks in his little lips and his eyes move rapidly under their translucent lids. He has long, dark eyelashes. His thatch of dark hair is sticky with sweat. His breathing is rapid and rhythmic, his little tummy rising and falling, up and down, up and down. A shred of gauze quivers on what is left of his umbilical cord. His pink, dry skin is almost purple around the knees and in the folds of his neck. His little feet stick up into the air, motionless.

Observing him from the side like that, he looks dead and S. quickly turns her head away.

This is supposed to be her son. She gave birth to him that afternoon at the Karolinska Hospital in Stockholm. But to her this is simply a nameless little being who after nine months has come out of her body. Nothing connects them anymore. S. feels relieved at the thought. She is free. Her entire past has spilled out of her body with this child. She feels so light, as if she could get up this very moment and walk away.

She is not alone in the room. Maj occupies the other bed. The woman turns to her and says, my name is Maj. S. does not reply. Maj is nursing her baby. She has enormous white breasts and as she pushes the nipple into the baby's mouth she looks as if she is going to smother it. Every so often the baby pulls away from the nipple, waving its little arms angrily and grimacing. Maj then props it up against her shoulder, smiles and looks at S. She does not smile back. She thinks how her own life is so very different. Maj, at least, is in her own country. S. is from Bosnia and that is like having no country. Maj's baby, a little girl, already has a name. She is called Britt. She also has a father and they know his first name and last, his occupation, the colour of his eyes, his habits. Maj's baby has everything: a family, a language, a country, security. The little being S. has given birth to has none of that.

S. does not pick the child up. She does not want to touch it. If she were to touch it even once she would become responsible for it. Like finding a stray kitten. As long as you do not pick it up off the ground you have nothing to do with it. But once you pick it up, that's it, it's yours . . .

She feels nothing but animosity toward this creature. The first thought that came to her mind when she realised that she was pregnant was death. This child was condemned to death from the start. It lived only because by that time it was already too late for an abortion. She had to carry through her pregnancy to the bitter end, with a swelling stomach that deformed her beyond recognition and made her hate her own body.

At breakfast that morning she had felt the first sharp piercing pain in her stomach. But she was not afraid of the labour pains; she welcomed them. She could hardly wait to get rid of her burden. She was used to the pain of being hit by a rifle butt, slapped, tied up, to the dull pain of her head being banged against the wall, of being kicked in the chest by a boot. Then the kind of pain from which you pass out, the pain that one body inflicts on another, the pain you feel when somebody else is in pain. And finally, the pain you simply stop feeling.

She welcomed this particular pain with a certain sense of relief. For the past few months she had been living like a vegetable, benumbed, waiting to give birth. This was something real, something sharp that snapped her out of her deadness and reminded her for a moment that she did exist.

While her body was being wracked with the agonies of labour, S. kept thinking that she had to hold on just a little longer. Her life was going to change. She would forget, forget the summer of 1992. The nurse was saying something to her, perhaps she was telling her to relax or to push harder, it was all the same to S. She did not hear her. The nurse would not be able to help her anyway. S. did not think anyone could.

Then she saw the doctor leaning over her and felt the touch of her hand on her face. It's over, said the doctor. That was the first tender touch she had had from an unfamiliar human hand in a long time. Only then did S. relax and cry. All the accumulated pain inside her slowly trickled out with her tears, and with the blood which was still flowing between her trembling legs.

And then peace. She no longer felt any pain. Half-asleep, she was roused by the nurse who brought over the baby, holding it upside down by its feet. S. made out the shape of an elongated, blood-streaked little body. It made no sound and S. thought that perhaps her wish had been granted and the baby was stillborn after all. That very same moment she heard it cry. She turned her head away. The baby's cry was no concern of hers. It had nothing to do with her any more.

Even before giving birth she had told them that she did not want to see the child. G., who had accompanied her to the hospital, had repeated S.'s request several times and the nurse at the admissions desk had duly noted it down. Just in case (what case? in case they did not believe her?), she had brought along a copy of the letter from the psychologist explaining S.'s decision to give the child up for adoption because she was not psychologically ready to take care of it.

S. believed she was quite prepared for life after giving birth, however. She had had time to think during these past few months. She had made a bargain with herself: she would give birth to the baby provided she never saw it again. That seemed to be the best, the most rational solution for them both. Since she had been unable to abort. Or to finish the child off with her own hands.

She looks at the little creature sleeping and thinks of F. When F. gave birth at the refugee camp in Zagreb, S. happened to be there with her. There had been eight of them in that cramped little room with its iron bunk-beds. F. had picked up the pillow herself and placed it over the baby. It was a little girl, S. remembers. She had not even washed the blood off the child; that is what S. held against her the most. The woman from the next bed had cut the umbilical cord with an ordinary knife and F. had simply pressed the pillow down on the baby, covering it completely. After about ten minutes she said, it's over. Then the woman from the next bed picked up the limp little body and put it in a blue plastic grocery bag. S. never saw what she did with the bag. F.'s face revealed nothing but exhaustion. Later she got up and washed the blood-stained pillow-case herself.

Perhaps S. could do the same thing. Press down gently and it would all be over in a second, both her suffering and his. The baby is sleeping so peacefully, she is sure he would not feel a thing. She reaches down, almost touching him, feels the warmth of his skin and sees how his ribcage flutters with the beating of his heart. Abruptly she withdraws her hand as if afraid of burning it.

No, she could not do it. She has seen so much death that the very thought of it makes her sick. Worst of all, death has a smell all of its own. It is not the smell that is usually associated with dying and that makes people's skins crawl: the smell of freshly spilled animal blood, rotten meat, old age, illness or decay. It is not one of natural dying, but of violent, sudden death, of the moment when one feels one is dying but does not yet believe it, not quite. It does not last long. The smell of deathly fear starts spreading from the still living person the moment the entire body knows that this is the end, although the mind keeps on hoping. It is this clash that produces the stench of death, so pungent and repellent. Once you have been near it, it is difficult to forget. Once dead, the person develops a completely different stench, sweetish, like that of nauseating decay.

Earlier, before everything that happened this past year, she used to think she would have a baby one day. Now that seems to her like a different time, so far removed that it has nothing to do with her own life. She can no longer be sure of anything; least of all can she rely on such a distant memory. That was in those long-gone times, when there was still a connection between one's life and one's desires and decisions.

In the meantime, her life has become something different, unrecognisable. Or perhaps unimaginable. Lying in her hospital bed in Stockholm she still does not know what to call it, although she knows that the word already exists and that the word is: war. But for her, war is merely a general term, a collective noun for so many individual stories. War is every individual, it is what happened to that individual, how it happened, how it changed that person's life. For her, war is this child she had to give birth to.

From the day she learned that she was pregnant, there was nothing she hated more than this creature. Who knows if it would ever have survived her hatred had she not wound up in this hospital? S. herself found it hard to live with. Tossing and turning in bed at night, feeling this foreign body moving inside her belly, she would see their faces looming over her, the faces of the men, of his fathers. Nameless men, usually drunk. She did not know how many, but here and there she did remember a face, eyes, a voice, hands, a smell, often a stench. Any one of them could be the father.

They come to her in her sleep. They do not leave her alone; even here in Sweden they return, like lost luggage arriving on her heels. She often dreams the same dream: she is walking down a street in a strange town. Suddenly she catches sight of a familiar face. She is sure it is one of them. She always has a knife with her in this dream. She walks up to him and stabs him in the stomach, making sure that he gets a good look at her face first. As the knife plunges into him, she feels relieved, even happy. But she sees only surprise in his eyes. The man does not recognise her and is surprised that an utterly strange woman should deal him a lethal blow. S. cries in fury that he did not recognise her as his victim and that her revenge is pointless.

When this being, the fruit of their seed, started growing inside her it was like a tumour. S. fought this alien body, the sick cells that multiplied inside her against her will. She had read somewhere that by visualising cancer cells you could arrest their growth. But she felt that the tumour was growing rapidly. When she shut her eyes she saw the foreign cells quite clearly, multiplying, occupying her from within. She saw herself as an enormous receptacle whose sole purpose of existence was to feed the voracious clusters of cells. The image drove her crazy.

Now the tumour is beside her, as if transformed by some miracle into a child. It is difficult for S. to accept. She has never thought of it as a child, only as a disease, a burden she wished to get rid of, a parasite she wanted removed from her organism. She is horrified by the thought that all this time, all these nine long months, it was growing inside her against her will. That, in spite of her, it had clung to the walls of her womb until the end, that it had been born, that it had survived. Just like her.

Now that she has rid herself of the child's weight, her still weary body feels somehow unencumbered, if that can be said of flesh, bones and skin. But she is still bothered by this sense of being split in two. She does not yet feel that she is in possession of her body, that she is in complete control of it, that she is now herself. Perhaps she will have to live like that, with this crack that cannot be closed.

Again she is obsessed with a sense of dirtiness. This is another feeling she often has, and it is just as disturbing as her dream of revenge. She looks at her hands, at the dirt under her fingernails, at her smelly armpits, at her skin which is peeling away in tiny, almost invisible scales, at the thin layer of dust that is like a second skin. She knows she will never be clean again. No amount of water is enough. She drags herself out of bed and goes into the bathroom. She stands behind the blue shower curtain and lets the jet run over her face for a long time. The bathrooms here have no bath tubs, only a metal semi-circular rod with a curtain and a drain on the floor for the water. She sits down on the plastic chair beneath the shower, feels the water pellet her shoulders and breasts. A long, hot shower that gives her a feeling of luxury.

She watches the light trickle of blood run from between her legs and colour the water. She feels as if trickling out with it is something painful and heavy which hid inside her all these months. As if washing her from within, the water helps her to forget.

Looking at herself in the mirror, she sees that her face has not changed. Nothing can be seen on it, this is a clear, unmarked, ordinary face. She looks pale and has circles under her eyes, that is all. The first time she took a good look at herself in a mirror after her ordeal was when they arrived in Zagreb. She was in a common bathroom, she remembers the moment precisely. The only light came from a naked bulb and in that yellowish semi-darkness she saw her face. The same smooth skin, the same fawn-like eyes, straight eyebrows and full mouth.

At first S. did not like the fact that her face did not show how much she had changed. How could you survive what she had gone through and have it leave no external trace, mark you only from within? Were these traces really so invisible, or was it simply a matter of knowing how to read them? But now, looking at herself in the hospital bathroom, she feels it is better that nothing shows. It is better that all traces of suffering have been removed from the surface. It will protect her. With an innocent face like this it will be easier for her to lie to people about herself.

She takes immense pleasure in opening the jar of face cream. How wonderful it is to have face cream and a mirror again. And a face in the mirror. Is that what the future looks like?

When did she realise that there is a future after all? Perhaps the moment that she reconciled herself to her own death. It dawned on her that death would be better and it was then that something inside her snapped. And quite unexpectedly, that moment of complete reconciliation opened her up to the future.

It is already over. She is lying on her back, her eyes shut. Her head is turned away. She does not want to look at his face. That is her only defence. She feels a dull pain but does not open her eyes. She does not move. She makes no sound. The soldier leans his boot down on her chest. Turn around, he orders her. S. turns her head to him but does not open her eyes. Not yet. Open your mouth, the soldier orders her again. S. opens her mouth. She feels the warm spurt of his urine on her face. Swallow it, he shouts. She has no choice. She swallows the briny liquid. It seems to last forever and all she wants to do is die.

A man in a wheelchair is slowly moving from one end of the courtyard to the other, a blue-caped nurse walking beside him. The air is crisp, almost like in the mountains of Bosnia. For an instant she feels so lonely that she would gladly go down to the courtyard and sit in that wheelchair, just to have someone walk beside her.

She looks at this child who is no longer a part of her, whose future does not belong to her. In that instant S. believes that she is completely divested of any responsibility for him, but all the same she is glad that she gave birth to him, that she gave him life rather than death. How easy it is to forget that death also marks the person who causes it, she thinks to herself.

She feels a sudden pressure in her breasts, her night gown is wet. Her milk is flowing. She sits down confused, not knowing what to do. She had not counted on this. She takes a towel and shoves it under her night gown. What is going to happen with all this milk now?

Village of B., Bosnia

END OF MAY 1992

The smell, the smell of dust in the dry air, that is what she will remember. The taste of coffee with too much sugar. The image of women quietly climbing on to the bus, one by one, as if going on an excursion. And the smell of her own sweat. The bus drives off and suddenly S. is bathed in sweat, the perspiration breaking out on her face, under her arms, on her stomach, between her legs. She feels uneasy. Yes, perhaps this feeling of physical uneasiness is what she will remember most. That is the first sign that her body no longer belongs to her alone, and hereafter she will have to bear that in mind . . .

It is late in the afternoon. The air in the bus is stuffy. S. finds it hard to breathe, closed in by the stench of human fear. The women are cramped together, sitting even in the aisle between the two rows of seats. Peering out between their feet, bags, bundles and plastic bags of food is the rusty tin floor. The perspiring head of the child next to her hangs from its mother's arm as if about to drop off at any minute.

S. unglues herself from the plastic seat and squeezes through to the window. She leans over and looks toward the village. Behind the bend she sees the outlines of the last houses. The sky has already turned dark with smoke. The village is desolate now, empty of people. Only the animals remain. Her orange cat, the sparrows she fed on the window sill and the chained village dogs. The soldiers will take away the cows and pigs, S. thinks to herself, and the thought consoles her somehow. She returns to her seat. She knows that if she turns around once more she will see nothing but that whirl of smoke screening the sun, and that soon she will start doubting the very existence of the village of B., her life, her very self . . . everything she had been so sure of until that summer day of 1992.

It was in the morning that she had first heard the voices. Yes, sometime that morning, even though normal time stopped when she stepped on to the bus.

Still half-asleep, she hears them, male voices, swearing and shouting. She opens her eyes. She sees the white curtain on her window billowing in the breeze, and the blue bedroom wall, and for a moment that restores her self-confidence. But these strange, foreign voices are getting closer. The curtain is expanding, as if it has lungs. The cool air caresses her skin. Birds are chirping in the cherry tree next door, for an instant drowning out the human noise. If she gets up and leans out of the window S. will see where these voices are coming from, who these people passing through the village in the early morning are. But S. does not want to do that. She does not want to wake up completely. Maybe whatever is going on outside has nothing to do with her at all. She quickly falls asleep again, hoping the noise will disappear.

A little later, she is awakened by the voice of her neighbour in the house across the street. Don't, she is saying to somebody, pleading at first and then sobbing. Her voice is quite clear, as if she were standing right here in the room, separated by nothing but the whiteness of the curtain. The man with whom she is pleading and whom she obviously knows, swears violently. Where are the weapons, where did you hide them, where's your husband, he shouts. His voice is drowned out by her sobs.

The soldiers go from house to house. They are searching. They say they are looking for weapons, but who knows what they are really looking for. S. stands behind the curtain and watches two strange men in uniform walk down the street. They are leading an elderly man, dressed in civilian clothes. He lives alone and is ill. S. knows him. She sees one of them step into the courtyard and pull the gold chain from the neck of the woman standing there. Maybe that is what they really are, ordinary robbers pretending to be some sort of army. She tries to remember where she put her jewellery; they may leave her alone if she gives it to them right away. She is only a woman, after all.

Then three buses arrive. They pull up in front of the school where she lives and teaches. Three orange buses with grey markings on the side. A group of men alight from one of them. A few are wearing camouflage uniforms, the rest are not in uniform. They all have rifles. They spread out through the village.

Time passes but no one has appeared at her door as yet. Still, S. does not dare leave the school building. She still thinks that, except for the jewellery, there is nothing for them to find in her place. She thinks the soldiers will pass her by.

Then, just as she is making herself a coffee, she hears a commotion on the stairs and the shuffling of feet in front of the door to her apartment. S. knows that it is them and that it is too late. She feels as if she has missed the last train or failed to do something important, although she does not know exactly what that could be. It is only then that it occurs to her that she could have fled. That morning she could still have gone down into the courtyard, taken her bicycle and headed for the road. Perhaps she could have left even earlier, when the shooting had started in Sarajevo. Why had she stayed in the village? Why had she waited, what had she been hoping for?

She feels a tightness in her throat. Suddenly the door is

kicked open. It was not locked, anyway. She had not even locked the door, that is how naïve she is. *That wouldn't have helped me anyway*, S. thinks to herself, lying in the hospital in Stockholm. *I go back to that moment for the nth time, and I'm still not sure that I understand how it all happened.*

Standing at the door is a young man. He looks certain that she is waiting for him. S. is standing in the kitchen by the stove. She turns around and stops in mid-motion. She says not a word. We'll collect all the people right here, the young man says quite loudly, although she asks him nothing. He does not say which people or why. This, she guesses, is supposed to serve as an explanation. S. is surprised that the young man does not shout louder and that he offers any explanation at all, rather than just the commands she is expecting. He is tall and thin, with long arms. He is wearing dirty camouflage pants and an undershirt. The black nail of his big toe is poking out of his torn cloth sneakers. S. notices the first traces of a moustache on the boyish face topping the long neck.

S. is still standing next to the stove as if paralysed. She does not dare move or speak. She realises that what she is looking at here is the face of war. Somebody simply opens the door of your apartment and war enters your life, enters you. She knows that from this moment on, there are no more obstacles standing between her and war.

He sizes her up. She does the same. Will he hit her? Will he ask for the jewellery? In the meantime she has found the little jewellery box and placed it within reach. The young man does not look dangerous, in spite of the rifle he is holding. He even seems to be blushing with embarrassment. Perhaps in his previous life someone had taught him to knock at the door first, because it is rude to burst into somebody else's apartment. Perhaps that is what he is thinking when he walks into the little kitchen with its smell of coffee, but he promptly forgets it. Now that he has a rifle, he no longer needs to knock. He sees the girl staring at him, her body tense. He considers pointing his gun to frighten her even more. But he changes his mind, he slowly lifts the rifle toward his shoulder, then changes his mind again, and lowers it. S. does not move and he is satisfied. S. opts for a cautious smile.

Sit down, S. finally manages to say, do you want some coffee? She does not know what else to say. What she would really like to say is: I have nowhere to run, what's all the rush? Quite unexpectedly, the young man accepts her invitation. He sits down. He props his rifle between his knees. He does not dare lean it against the wall. She sits down as well, facing him. He sips the freshly made coffee unhurriedly, as if the goings-on outside the kitchen have little to do with him. The coffee is hot and too sweet. She thinks she is perfectly calm, but she was perturbed enough to put too much sugar in the coffee. Now she wonders whether he will notice her agitation. But he simply sips his coffee in silence, as if absent from the situation.

To this day I am not sure why I offered him a cup of coffee, maybe I felt sorry for him, he was so child-like and gawky. I didn't take him seriously yet, maybe because of his sneakers.

For a moment, everything is peaceful. The silence makes S. feel uneasy. For a moment she thinks of asking him to explain. Why? Just that one solitary question crouching inside her, coiled like a wild animal ready to pounce. What would happen if she were to ask it now, if she were finally to ask it? S. looks at the young man sitting across from her. His forehead is pimply. The hand holding the porcelain cup so awkwardly is strong and rough. It was probably holding a shovel only yesterday. If she were to ask that question, absolutely nothing would happen. It would be left to hang in the air between them. He would not understand it and would be furious that she had dared to ask him anything. S. would regret ever having asked it. Anyway, she had spent that whole morning guessing the answer.

The young man's cup is empty. He is a soldier, after all, not your regular visitor, and he decides to prove it to her. He gets up and fingers his rifle. Pack your things, he says formally, you're taking a trip. S. notices that he addresses her with the formal *Vi*, perhaps because he knows that she is a teacher. The peasants all address her with *ti*. Maybe he left school only recently, she thinks to herself, and the thought brings a smile to her face.

A trip? Naturally, he does not tell her where she is going or why she should be going on a trip in the first place.

People are already beginning to arrive in the gym on the ground floor. She hears them calling out to each other. S. thinks of the scene she saw on television last night, a busload of children leaving the war-afflicted area. Among them were babies. The women touched the glass of the windows, crying. The children waved. It had seemed to be happening somewhere else, and to someone else. Who knows why, but she thought something like that would not happen in this mountain village. Maybe that is what everybody thinks until it happens to them.

Rumours had already been spreading that the army was nearing the village. Some villagers sent their children off to relatives in Germany. She had been against that, the school year was not yet over. *I told the parents that I would not be able to give their children their end of term grades. Who knows where they are today, or if they are alive?* Some left themselves, thinking that it was only temporary and that they would be back once the situation calmed down. But the majority stayed. They had nowhere else to go. The men kept saying that they had nothing to fear, that they had always lived together with the Serbs, that they had no weapons anyway and that the army would establish peace. There were not many men in the village and most of them were elderly. The young ones were working in Slovenia or in towns across Bosnia. There was still no shooting in the area. They did not really believe that this was war, the beginning of war, not even when you couldn't travel. And then the buses arrived.

The young man does not tell her, of course, where the buses will take them or how long the journey will take. She is certain that he has no idea himself. He just keeps telling her to hurry up, the buses are waiting. His voice sounds harsher with every word he utters. Soon he will start shouting, S. thinks to herself, trembling.

How else can you think about leaving home except as going on a trip? S. has to believe that she will return, even if she is thinking merely of her temporary place of residence. It is not easy to uproot a person. People are like plants. S. feels how tightly she is holding on to the familiarity of that reality, how she is clinging to things, to the land, to other people, to their language. She cannot even imagine at that moment that this barefaced young man is moving her out, not only from her apartment but from her country which, until he had stepped into her kitchen, she had thought of as being both his country and hers.

Through the open door of the room she sees her unmade bed and soft pillow, still bearing the impression of her head. The curtain is still billowing. S. feels as if neither this room nor the bed have any purpose in her life any more. She is fully aware that there is absolutely nothing she can do to change her situation.

How much time does she have to get ready? An hour? Five minutes? She walks around the apartment in an uncertain frame of mind. What should she take when she does not know where she is going? What kind of clothes? Just summer clothes or winter clothes as well? And what about books? Is there any point in taking along some books? She is sorry to leave the books and new stereo system behind. When you go on a trip, you know where you are going and when you are coming back, so you know exactly what to take along. But this is no ordinary trip. S. instinctively knows that she will not see this apartment, school or village for a long time. She thinks to herself that maybe she will not need anything wherever it is they are being taken to. Then she quickly suppresses this ominous thought.

She tries to be calm and collected. She should take with her only the bare essentials. They will probably put them in some sort of refugee centre. It cannot be for long. Or maybe they will immediately send them across the border, to Croatia, or even further. If there is a way, she will look for her relative in Zagreb. Nothing terrible has happened yet, which is why she tries to act as rationally as possible. She takes her blue canvas backpack which she usually carries on school excursions. From the drawers in her bedroom she takes some underwear, a few summer tops, a shirt, a sweater. She also puts into her backpack a photograph album, a jewellery box containing a gold chain, a pair of earrings and a medallion, an empty notebook and two ballpoint pens. Then there is her toothbrush and a tube of toothpaste, some soap, face cream and two packets of sanitary napkins and an extra package of cotton wool, which is all she has in the house at the moment. She cannot think what else she may need on this journey into the unknown.

If it were some earlier year, and not 1992, she would soon be getting ready in much the same way to go on summer vacation. First there would be the bus and then a boat. It had been like that last summer. She thinks of the coast. Every year she would spend the summer with her friends in M., where the boughs of the pine trees graze the water's surface. When they swam at night their bodies would gleam like fish. She remembers B., the touch of his lips on her shoulder, and how he had slipped his hand through the opening in her dress and fondled her breasts. And later, the smell of his skin on the sheets. B., too, had been swept up by this maelstrom, but earlier. Even while they were on vacation, some were called up into the army. The shooting had already started in Croatia, but the two of them swam, grilled fish over a fire and did not believe any of it. They thought it was all far removed from them and not their concern. *As if we were deliberately blind, we thought we could defend ourselves against the horror by not seeing it. By not looking . . .*

B. has not been in touch with her for months and S. does not know where he is. She wrote to his mother not long ago but has not yet received an answer. At first, after that summer vacation, they had phoned each other often, assuring one another that it was all a lot of nonsense, that there would be no war in Bosnia. Then they somehow lost touch, as if they had been overwhelmed by that same lot of nonsense themselves.

His letters are already stowed away in the pocket of her backpack, but it occurs to S. that wherever they are going, somebody might read them. The thought is unbearable. She takes out the letters and sets a match to them over the sink. The letters burn quickly. Finally, she turns on the tap and lets the water wash away the ashes.

She feels a kind of disbelief rather than sadness, as if she is still not certain that this is all happening to her. She knows that she is rambling around the apartment, picking things up. At the same time, however, she feels as if the real S. is standing off to the side, quietly watching her.

S. looks one last time around the apartment. What else can she take? Her backpack is half-empty. She takes her red summer dress and a new pair of Italian shoes from the wardrobe, her two best possessions. The shoes still smell of fine leather.

Then she goes downstairs. As she closes the apartment door behind her she feels that her life has been emptied of all its normality.

The gym is stuffy. People are sitting on the benches lining the walls and on the floor. The men are smoking and it is already clouding the air. There are about a hundred people here in all. Among them are a handful of schoolchildren from the village; the other children would come to school on foot or by bus from the surrounding hamlets. Standing guard at the door is a man with a machine-gun and two cartridge belts slung across his bare chest. He is wearing a woollen cap and keeps wiping the sweat off his brow. Some twenty armed men are assembled in a corner of the gym. Only a handful of them are in the familiar olive-green army uniform, the rest are wearing civilian clothes. They are drinking beer. S. recognises the policeman from the next village and the mailman. The mailman waves at her. He still has his mailman uniform on, but now he has a pistol hanging from his belt. The young man who had burst into her apartment is sitting on an overturned beer crate. He beckons her over. He tells her that since she is a teacher, she will keep an eye on the women. He is gruff with her in front of the other men, and now uses the familiar *ti* when speaking to her. His voice is deeper, as befits someone giving orders. S. sees that he feels proud to be in the dangerous company of adult men. Keep an eye on them, what do you mean? S. asks him. You know, that they all get on the bus, that nobody hides, says the young man, pointing to his rifle. S. ignores the gesture. She thinks to herself how unnecessary this warning is; who would want to stay alone in the village and where would they hide? But she does not say this aloud.

Already I was swallowing not only my words, but even my thoughts; the silence I was soon to submerge myself in, like the peasants around me, was already beginning.

A strange stillness reigns in the gym for a while. To S. it is as if a kind of stupor has taken hold of the people, as if they are not quite aware of what is happening to them. It is stuffy with cigarette smoke, but nobody dares to open a window. A baby is crying, but the cry is muffled, as if its mother is holding it tightly against her chest. The boy next to her asks his mother softly who these people are. The woman squeezes his hand and puts her finger to her lips. S. notices how his eyes open wide with fear.

She sees a fat man in camouflage uniform with a belt slicing through his stomach appoint a group of men to search the basements and attics. Then a man with a beard orders all the men to one side. There is a commotion in the gym. There are maybe some twenty men in this group of villagers, most of them elderly. S. sees her neighbour who is hunched over with rheumatism and can no longer stand up straight, and with him his deaf father to whom she used to bring pills for his blood pressure. The soldiers will not let them sit down or lean against the wall. Then a little girl runs towards her father and hangs on his arm. The soldier pushes her away with his rifle. The little girl falls on to the parquet floor and lies there curled into a ball, crying. Her father steps out of the group and bends down over her. Then that same soldier whacks him in the back with his rifle butt. S. sees the blow coming. It seems to her slow, very slow. She hears a muffled echo. It is the only sound, apart from the girl's crying. Suddenly there is absolute silence in the gym, the silence that comes with fear. Terror creeps into the people and nestles inside them, there to remain.

The small group of men is being led out of the gym. They are escorted by five armed men in civilian clothes and a policeman. To her it looks like some kind of established procedure or operation in which both the armed and separated group of men know what is happening and why. No one asks any questions. No one resists. Why not? It is as if they are all in a state of numbness. Is it because of the stuffy air, because of the mugginess? Or do the men now being led out think this must be some sort of mistake which someone will rectify any minute? They should say they are innocent. They have no weapons. They did not shoot at any soldiers, they did not shoot at anyone. But they have to say it now, while they are still in the gym. They say nothing and leave. These people seem to her unable to understand that for these armed men they are guilty simply because they exist, because they are different, because they are Muslims. And that that is reason enough for them . . .

Later, S. is no longer sure. She thinks that they understood what was happening much better than she did, and that was why they said nothing. They knew what was going to happen, she was the one who didn't.

She herself feels present one moment and absent the next; she can hear the beating of her own heart, but she can neither move nor speak.

After some twenty minutes, perhaps more, there is the distant muted sound of gunfire. Each shot is distinct and the boy beside her flinches with every one. A woman nearby covers her mouth with her hand in a silent scream. S. stares at the floor, she does not dare look at the faces around her.

The armed men return alone and go back to drinking their beer, as if they had finished a difficult job. They guzzle the liquid down with avid enjoyment. S. observes their bobbing Adam's apples, their rapacious greed, their thirst. The feeling that she is attending something unreal grows. Just a while ago, those men, her acquaintances and neighbours, had been together in the gym with them. Now they are gone.

They left and disappeared. S. is appalled by the nearness of death. She feels nauseous. She walks up to the guard at the door. She asks him if she can go to the toilet. The toilet is cold and smells of chlorine. S. kneels down on the familiar concrete floor and throws up. She washes her face. She is breathing more easily now. She walks over to the window and inhales deeply. There is the smell of dust. An abandoned dog is whining in the courtyard next door.

Now they are being taken to the buses. They do not have their names written down or called out, nor are their papers checked. S. cannot explain this to herself, unless the armed men are certain that everybody in this village is of the same nationality and the same fate awaits them all, regardless of their names. The women climb on to the bus slowly, one by one. They stand in line. They wait patiently as if something is about to be handed out. It is their submissiveness that shocks S. more than anything else, their willingness to obey orders without question. She thinks this is so, not only because the men have guns, but also because these people are still in a state of disbelief, in some temporary state of numbness, that they refuse to understand what is happening to them. Or perhaps it is a kind of naivety, the belief that surely somebody must know what is being done and why, that there must be a reason for this action. S. is unable to discern what is really happening herself. Later she recognises such behaviour as a result of fear, which paralyses the whole being—thought, movement and emotion.

A youngish woman, who worked in the village store, faints in front of the bus. Her husband was in the group of men that was just taken out and shot. S. bends down and lays the woman's head in her lap. She is pale and her forehead is cold to the touch. Her breathing is barely audible. S. undoes the belt on her dress. The woman is wearing a flowery light blue summer dress, one of her best. S. feels like bursting into tears at the sight of this silky dress and the woman laid out in the dust. Someone brings over a bottle of water and the woman drinks from it. S. brushes the dirt off the dress and puts her in the front seat of the bus. The woman does not open her eyes, as if her closed lids are her last defence against the truth.

Let's go, somebody shouts, and the buses move off. There are four soldiers in each. Some sit among the blankets, pillows, plastic bags and suitcases . . . the vestiges of a normal life. These people are leaving behind uneaten food on the table, unwashed dishes, unfinished work, animals in the barn, radios playing, laundry for ironing, arguments. S. barely manages to squeeze her way to her seat at the back of the bus. Sitting next to her is an old woman; she knows her, she must about ninety. The old woman pats S. on the hand. Don't be afraid, dear, she says, we're still alive. I'm not afraid, says S. What other answer can she give her right now?

S. dozes off. She is dazed by the heat and fatigue. She leans her shoulder against the old woman's head. Her black clothes smell of old age and burned milk.

S. is very little, maybe about three years old. A big red pot sits on the old-fashioned stove. The milk in it is boiling. She watches the milk simmer, boil and rise to the rim of the pot. Grandma, she cries, grandma. Her grandmother runs in but it is already too late, the milk is spilling over the rim of the pot. It leaves an ugly brown stain on the surface of the stove. The smell of burned milk fills the kitchen. S. stands on the chair by the stove and leans to look in the pot. Her thigh touches the hot rim. The pain is so great she does not manage even to cry out. The smell of the burned milk blends with that of her burned skin. She can still feel the scar on her thigh even now.

The camp, Bosnia

END OF MAY 1992

S. cannot say how long they were on the road. She remembers that they stopped twice somewhere by the roadside. There are no houses around, just woods. And it is dark, the hills cast huge black shadows. The women step out into the night, run to the woods and immediately come back. They call out to each other, like children on an excursion, afraid they will get lost. None of them, evidently, sees this as a chance to escape.

It is night-time when they arrive at the camp. The buses pull up in front of a barbed wire fence at the end of the white road. The yellow moon grazes the nearby woods, illuminating the path, courtyard and several buildings, the closest of which looks like a warehouse. Darkness surrounds them. The hills and forbidding woods loom black. She hears the voice of a man (a soldier? a guard?) tell somebody that this is an exchange camp. Right now the word exchange sounds soothing, almost believable. Others too are relieved that this is the end of the journey. They have arrived, even if it is in some sort of factory warehouse. S. bases this judgement on the tone of the voices around her. They can finally stretch their legs, which they see as a plus. A plus? *In a single day we had all been reduced to the lowest possible denominator, to brute existence.*

Together with the other women she enters a huge, dark room. She touches the floor: concrete. Then she lies down on it, placing her backpack under her head. Without a word, the women around her lie down too, as if they find it normal to lie down on bare concrete and go to sleep. Again that feeling that people are behaving as if what is happening to them has some deeper significance, but it looks as though she alone seems unable to decipher what it is. Is it because they can do nothing but adapt to the situation? S. had learned to ask questions. Still, in this new situation she decides to behave like the people around her and not to stand out in any way. I am hiding in the crowd for the first time, S. thinks to herself. The only difference between her and the women around her is that S. knows it.

She is awake. Again she thinks about fear. Until then, she had not been aware of fear, she had been convinced that she did not feel fear, not even when they had taken the group of men out from the gym, or when she had heard the burst of gunfire. She listens. She knows now that fear is the absence of all emotion, it is emptiness, it is as if your whole body is drained of blood all at once.

The day seems to have gone by so quickly and the turn of events has left her no time to think. The young man's appearance at her apartment that morning had marked the beginning of a different life, and S. is afraid that soon she will no longer be able to compare or connect those two lives . . .

She lies like that for a while, watching to see whether the thin stream of light filtering in from the crack in the roof will spread. She listens to the sleeping bodies and the quiet makes her skin crawl. She does not hear any children crying. Perhaps they are not crying because they already know that it is pointless, because they have been struck dumb with fear. Sometimes children know more than adults, S. thinks to herself as her weary body falls asleep against her will.

She wakes up. Her limbs feel heavy, as if glued to the floor. Although she feels that this is her body, she does not feel entirely present in the warehouse, in the camp, stretched out between two unfamiliar bodies. As if the bus had transported only a part of her. For the first time she clearly notices this disparity, a kind of discomfort and partition. She senses a crack inside her, the starting line of this separation. She tries to take her mind back to her apartment in the school, but to no avail. She is not sure whether it is possible that she has already forgotten her past, or whether this is some sort of defence against her premonition of the horror that is yet to come.

Whenever she slips in between two realities, she feels as if she does not exist. S. had already experienced this once during the trip. She had fallen asleep and when she arrived she thought she had never even left, but there she was, already at her destination. This absence from her familiar reality hit her like a mild dizzy spell. Even then she had had nothing to hold on to. The sight of the unfamiliar street had terrified her: she had not recognised a single shop window, sign, façade. For a moment she had been completely displaced. Now she recognises the same feeling. She tries to bridge the divide between the two realities by thinking logically: perhaps their stay in the camp will be brief, perhaps they will be exchanged as early as tomorrow. She cannot imagine why the soldiers would hold so many women and children captive in a warehouse, in the dark, with no windows.

She is upset by the fact that the totality of the event still escapes her. Her mother, an employee with a state-owned company, is a Serb. Her father, an engineer, is a Muslim, which means that S. is neither one nor the other. That is why S. thinks she is exempt from alignment. This is what she believed until the armed men and soldiers arrived in her mountain village that same day. Now, however, she sees that for her war began the moment others started dividing and labelling her, when nobody asked her anything any more. If her father is a Muslim, to them she is a Muslim as well, and can be nothing else. Her mother does not count. Her picture of reality is shattering, as if the television screen had exploded that day and the war had simply spilled into her apartment. Now she herself is caught up in this rushing torrent. If she wants to survive, she will have to obey those who have the weapons. Her life, like her death, is no longer a matter of choice.

In the warehouse, lying full-length on the floor, S. consoles herself that nothing terrible has happened as yet, at least not to her. That very same instant she is horrified by her own thought, by the stupidity of it. Nothing? Armed men had come, and together with the soldiers they had assembled the people, separated and killed a group of men, herded the women on to buses and imprisoned them in a camp. They had torched the village. She thought of the woman who had fainted and of her cold forehead. Everything had already happened to her.

I am lying, lying to myself. Everything has happened to me as well, almost everything, S. thinks to herself. She can see her high-rise building in Grbavica in Sarajevo, the balconies whose blue paint had long since been washed away, the television aerials and clothes lines with the laundry hanging out. But she still cannot imagine that the night had devoured her parents and sister. *I should have found a way to get there, to get into Sarajevo and see for myself that they were no longer there.* Her friends had advised her to stay in the village, she would be safe there. This could not last long. Still, she had tried to leave as soon as she had heard. The bus had stopped after only an hour. They were told that the road was closed. S. returned to the village.

Their disappearance was still something remote and unreal to her. Like when the phone line suddenly goes temporarily dead, because of a storm. Only now does she see that the entire time she has been refusing to accept that they are really dead, taken away somewhere, and she cannot forgive herself. What was she thinking? That the news of their disappearance was a mistake or a bad joke? Had she gone, to see for herself, then perhaps the events of this morning would make more sense . . .

When she heard that they were gone she had wanted to die, as if death was something you could request. Why did it have to be her parents? Why her sister? If they had fled from Sarajevo she would have known it. Were they taken away simply because they had not left Grbavica on time and, like S., did not believe that what was happening all around them was really war?

When she shuts her eyes she can see her mother setting the table. She can hear the dishes rattling in the kitchen. Her father is already sitting at the table, her sister is opening the front door and smiling at them. Soon the three of them will be sitting down for dinner. Her father will be the first to go to bed. He is usually the first to get up in the morning and make the coffee for her mother. Her mother and sister will clean up the kitchen, and then watch some programme on television. The next morning they will not be in that apartment.

Only later did S. learn that there are countless kinds of pain, that physical pain usually passes and that you can distance yourself from it if you learn how. But she already knows that there is a certain kind of pain from which there is no escape, merely rest, sometimes. Her neighbour informed her that it had happened. She said that the apartment was empty, and later that a soldier had moved into it. She said that maybe her family was still alive, somewhere. S. realised that the neighbour was saying this just to make her feel better. The instant she said it, the pain inside her had contracted into something hard. And it had been there ever since, here inside her, she could almost feel it under her skin.

She remembered those words often. Maybe they are alive, maybe they will find a way to survive. Will she ever know? The only thing she has to hold on to is that slim hope, the neighbour's words, nothing more.

In her mind there are two clashing images: the past and the present. But trying to accustom herself to her place on the concrete floor between the two unfamiliar bodies, her previous life looks so remote to her that it is as if it had happened to somebody else and she is now watching the movie, recognising only bits of it: the glass of ice-cold Coke she drank in the outdoor restaurant that spring in Sarajevo; her sister's face as they walked on the sunny side of the Miljacka river and she told S. how she had fallen in love; their reflections in the shop window; the fruit stand on the corner of their street and how she would lean over to smell the first strawberries. How much longer would these memories last? Is it good to remember or is it easier to survive if you forget you ever lived a normal life?

There was not even a three-year age difference between S. and her sister. L. would always know how to make her feel better, she knew more about everything. About dolls. About shoes. About boys. She knew how to cajole their parents into letting them go to the Saturday night dance. L. also knew how to lie and that fascinated S. She kept the small change when she went to the store and later secretly bought cigarettes with it. Why didn't she, at least, leave Sarajevo? She had said she could not leave their parents alone. But S. had not believed her, not entirely. Her sister had stayed because of her boyfriend but had not admitted it, thinks S., still mad at her sister.

She has to get up and pee. Last night the guards showed them the bucket in the corner of the warehouse. She turns carefully on to her side and then gets up. It is already getting light. Lying on the floor on one side of her is a little girl in a thin dress, and on the other is an old woman, with a scarf on her head and thick woollen socks on her feet. Every so often the old woman releases a whistle-like sound through her nose. She has covered her face with the scarf and crossed her hands under her arms. The women lie pressed against one another on the bare floor as if the nearness of each other's bodies will protect them against misfortune. S. cannot make out their faces. In the semi-darkness not one of them seems to have a face of her own, they all look the same because whatever made each of them different was eradicated when they entered the camp.

To reach the bucket she has to walk along the wall, taking care not to stand on anybody's hand or foot. Slowly she makes her way, stepping over the bodies of the sleeping women and groping along the wall. She only hopes the bucket is not full. There is no lid on it and there is an unbearable stench coming from that side of the warehouse. The surrounding floor is wet with urine. When did they manage to make it so dirty? It never would have occurred to her that they would be put in a space without windows, without beds or toilets. But now she steers clear of such thoughts, which are dangerous for her because they are no longer applicable to her new situation. Since yesterday morning she has been trying not to let anything that is happening surprise her. It is too easy to lose oneself in pointless questions to which no one gives any answers.

It is still dark enough for her to be able to pee without humiliation. That is the whole point, the aim is to humiliate people. The internees cease to be human beings and their bodily needs, like their bodies themselves, become part of the machinery whose workings and aim they can only guess.

Returning to her spot by the same route, she hears a woman painfully sobbing in her sleep. The little girl turns on to her side, facing her. She smells of a child's sweat. S. lies down next to her, her body recognising her new bed. She places her arm under her head and surprises herself by how quickly she is adapting to the situation.

She feels the stirring of the women and hears the voices of men. The door of the warehouse is open and several guards are herding the women into the courtyard. Like dogs, they bark out their orders. For the first time she sees in the full light of day the warehouse in which they have spent the night. It is a long concrete building with an asbestos roof which is already absorbing the heat. She thinks that this must have been a warehouse for machines, because there are metal parts still strewn around.

The yard is divided into two by a fence. At the back, about fifty metres away, opposite the warehouse, is a white one-storey building. That is the administration building. She takes a quick look around; there is no sign of habitation, she sees not a single house. They could be anywhere; the camp looks utterly isolated. This only heightens her present sense of an unreal world, where it is truly possible to wake up and suddenly find yourself in a camp. The women say that close by, nearer the woods, is the men's camp. They say it is much bigger . . .

Now the guards herd them into the field behind the fence. At the entrance to the camp the guard lets through a group of some twenty women. There is no shelter in the field, no bush to hide behind and protect them from staring eyes. They simply have to crouch and defecate in a group, in the middle of the field, in front of the guards, in front of everyone.

S. is in the second group. For the first time she thinks of escape. All she would have to do is get up and run for the woods, run until she escapes or is stopped by a bullet. Maybe she would reach the woods. But S. is afraid of the woods, she is sure she would get lost in them. Helplessly she crouches down. She avoids looking around her. She remembers how she and her sister had once run into a field and crouched together to pee, laughing. The ground is dry and warm to the touch. She takes a clod of earth and crumbles it in her hand. She looks at this yellowish soil and sparse grass and does not dare to look up. She knows she is exposed and there is nothing she can do to protect herself, absolutely nothing.

The women are standing in the yard around the water tap; each one has a few minutes to wash and to drink water. Standing in front of S. is a woman with a child who is maybe three. The child drinks the water in long gulps, its eyes closed. Gleaming droplets of water slide down his chin and neck. Mama, the water is so good, says the child, wiping his mouth with his arm. His mother strokes his head.

Finally it is S.'s turn to let the water run over her face. She is dirty from the trip, from the bus. And she is tired. It is still morning but the heat is already burning the concrete in the yard. She does not know the exact time. Her mother's little gold watch is gone. It was a graduation present. A drunken soldier had turned the light on in their bus and started collecting rings and bracelets, anything that was made of gold. Gold in the sun, he shouted. He held a cap in one hand and a bottle of brandy in the other. S. undid her watch strap and dropped the watch into the greasy cap. When it fell on to the little pile of gold jewellery it was as if it was falling into a timeless zone where watches served no purpose anyway. Later she noticed the soldier divvy up his booty with the driver and both of them looked pleased.

She swallows the water with her eyes closed until her teeth go numb from the cold. She is suffused with a feeling of calm. Only she, the water and this moment exist. She feels her body, cold skin, muscles, her thirst, her body's joy to be alive. Perhaps this is the only way to survive, by living from one moment to the next. The continuous flow of time no longer exists for her, merely isolated moments which are impossible to weave into a meaningful whole.

A hand shoves her aside. This time it is not the guard, it is the woman standing in line behind her. The woman throws her a hard, angry look, as if S. has just stolen something from her.

The guards distribute food in plastic buckets: two slices of bread and a piece of salami. She feels sick at the sight of the salami and gives hers to the boy next to her. His mother tells him, you have to share that with your sister, but it is too late, the salami is already disappearing down the boy's throat. S. is shocked by his selfishness. His behaviour is beyond her because she has yet to learn what the little boy instinctively knows. This seven-year-old little boy has already learned the first lesson of survival in a camp—selfishness.

S. remembers the first days in the camp as a series of unconnected, brightly lit images. Even now, she can still call to mind certain faces and scenes which whirl in nightmarish disorder. She remembers the tense expectation that something was going to happen, that they would be going somewhere, that they would be exchanged, it was just a matter of hours. And the disbelief that she was going to remain there. Then the repetition of ordinary acts which ultimately mean that none of what they expect will actually happen, at least not soon.

Most of the women go under guard to dig in the nearby field. The children accompany them. Some of the women go to the kitchen; there is a lot of work in the kitchen, the food has to be prepared for the entire camp. Another group is assigned to do the cleaning. S. and E. are assigned to tend to the sick. At last she has some sort of task. She feels better immediately, less scared. She had feared idleness, feared she would be spending her days sitting on the concrete floor of the warehouse, waiting to be exchanged. That is the easiest way to lose your mind. As E.'s assistant, she can at least be of some use to someone. She knows E., a nurse who worked in the village's outpatient clinic. The woman is here with her twelve-year-old daughter; she had nowhere to send her, and she could not imagine being separated from her. She is S.'s pupil. A quiet girl, one of those who likes to read. She walks around the camp beside her mother with her head bowed, as if ashamed of something. She doesn't ask any questions, that's what I find the hardest says E., she has completely withdrawn into herself. If only she would at least talk. S. hugs the girl. She can feel the child's frail shoulders under her touch, the small bones, the spine. She is so thin, this little girl, so frail. S. feels she owes her some sort of explanation, but she cannot think of anything. She tells the girl that they will soon be leaving together for Zagreb and that once they get there she will take her to the movies. She looks at E., her hands are strong, her hair is pulled back to keep it out of the way. She looks robust, as if she can take anything. But how can one take this kind of responsibility? How can one protect one's child when war erupts?

In the warehouse a woman complains that she can't breathe, she has a weak heart and high blood pressure. She is still young, but her colour is pale and unhealthy, her fair hair is thin and her eyes are big. She was operated on a year ago. E. knows her, she went to her house in the village to change her bandages and give her injections. E. has brought with her whatever medicine she had in the house, but the stock will probably last her a week, no more. She strokes the woman's hair. She tells her everything will be all right. She has nothing to give but these words and the touch of her hand, and the young woman clings to them desperately.

An old woman has hurt her ankle and E. puts wild herbs on it and then sets it between two slats of wood. She has no instruments or drugs, or even bandages. She is used to working in the village clinic where the doctor drops by only occasionally, so she knows about medicinal herbs and herbal medicine. But now E. is helpless because she has not even that, she has nothing to help these women. They might as well have sent me out to dig, she says. She goes to look for the commander of the camp. The guard takes her to the administration building.

S. is left alone with a little girl who has a burning fever. She places a cold compress on the child's brow and gives her a lot of water to drink. Then she pulls a wet t-shirt over her head. Maybe that will help to bring the temperature down. She remembers that her mother used to do that sometimes when she or L. came down with a fever. She would dip an entire sheet into freezing cold water and then wrap it around her child's rigid body. S. remembers the icy touch of the linen sheet all over her skin and feeling that the burning fire inside her was finally dying down. Or her mother would rub her chest and limbs with alcohol or vinegar and then she would lie in bed breathing shallowly, dazed by the vapours, until she would fall asleep. The little girl closes her eyes now too. She is breathing more easily.

Perhaps she will not be able to bear it after all. The behaviour of these women. The camp. The horror. S. feels that she is weak and her own weakness makes her sick.

There must be some sort of makeshift clinic in the camp because one day E. brings a few bandages and sedatives. And the promise that soon she will also get some antibiotics and pain-killing injections. She has managed to obtain a thermometer, although even she thinks it senseless in a situation where there is no hope of getting any medicine for the sick and dying. She brings the whole lot in a small frayed doctor's bag. S. is puzzled. Where did the doctor come from? And why has he not visited the warehouse? E. looks down. She opens the bag; neatly laid out inside are a stethoscope, injections, scissors, bandages. She avoids S.'s eyes. She gives a dismissive wave of her hand. S. has the impression that E. knows far more than she is prepared to say. The bag obviously belonged to a doctor, a prisoner in the other camp. So it is true after all, there is a men's camp nearby. They don't tend to them there at all, says E. simply. They do not need a doctor any more.

But even after what had happened in my school I still did not entirely believe what she said.

E. examines the baby lying in its mother's lap. The mother, a young woman with a white scarf covering her head, looks at her expectantly. But the child is dead, it is too late to do anything. The mother does not realise this yet and is still hoping.

For one more moment, just one more, there will be a spark of life in her eyes. Then it will go out. S. watches the light in the mother's eyes slowly die out, her arms suddenly fall limp. The mother is overwhelmed with a pain for which there is no solace. What can S. or anyone tell a woman whose child has just died? Suddenly the woman's face darkens, as if the colour of her skin has suddenly changed or a dark shadow just crossed her face. S. sees the shadow of death. And she sees how each of these women, including herself, will be forced from now on to live under this menacing shadow.

In this place, death is not something remote or foreign. It is no longer an unexpected visitor, as it is in ordinary life. Death is a constant companion in their lives, like a reflection in the mirror you cannot wish away because it is always there, waiting for you.

The mother now has to be separated from the infant. The two women have to tear her from the dead body of her child whom she is clutching to her breast. S. tries to pry away her hands, but the woman is too strong. They wrestle silently for a moment. S. gives up. Why wrest the child away from her? The woman needs time to realise that they are surrounded by death, that this is what the camp fence defines, a demarcated territory where death reigns supreme.

One morning two guards appear with a sheet of canvas. And old army blankets. They are shabby and dirty and reek of motor oil. Perhaps they were used to cover the machines in this same warehouse. Now they are to serve as bedding for the women. And later? It is more than obvious that they will be staying in this warehouse for some time to come. To S. the blankets are proof that they might even see in the winter here. As if she has received an official written communication, she no longer has the slightest doubt. She says so to E.

She too is afraid that this is a bad omen, and there are more and more such omens, she says grimly.

Another change follows a few days later. S. notices scrawny men, dressed only in rag-like pants, digging a pit at the back of the women's part of the courtyard, right by the fence. She knows they are internees from the men's camp. Some of the women try to edge closer to them and glean news of their loved ones. This is an opportunity for them. The guards are also amenable to bribes. They will obtain information in return for money, gold jewellery or clothes. S. wonders what their information is worth, how reliable it is. Her neighbour from the warehouse says they are good folk who have been forced into being guards, some of them are 'our people', as she puts it. And she says that they can be believed and that through them messages can even be sent to the men in the other camp.

Over the next few days, the detainees assemble a little wooden hut above the two pits. They are finally getting a toilet. It is now more than obvious that they will be staying in the camp, but S. is still glad about the toilet. To her, the advent of the toilet looks like major progress in their lives. If they have to live in this camp, at least they will no longer have to defecate out in the field, in front of everyone.

S. can feel herself adapting. Every day she wakes up to something she now recognises: the squeaking of the metal doors, the voices of the guards, the song of the birds, the whispering of the women around her. Before she gets up S. repeats to herself: just let this be a good day. She does not know exactly what good means, perhaps to her at that moment it means not to be exposed to humiliation by the guards. She learns quickly to ignore what does not directly concern her, not to think about tomorrow. She has learned that she can cope only with the problems of the here and now. She can focus on small tasks, such as how to obtain a bandage or wash something, when to grab a moment of rest without the guards seeing her. Anything else is beyond her.

She knows what to do, what is expected of her. She tries not to think about what is happening to others and tries not to believe the camp stories. They have food, a toilet, they sleep, nobody beats them. They still wash at the water tap in the courtyard. The heat is now unbearable and S. pours water over herself from head to toe at least once a day. She longs to bathe in a tub of water. She imagines there must be a bath somewhere in the camp, a shower at least, and that maybe she could bribe the guard to let her take a bath . . . No, it is better not to approach the guards, not to have anything to do with them. You never know how it will end. They do not need much of an excuse to whack somebody or do something even worse than that. It is better to become invisible. Indeed, S. notices that instinctively all the women abide by this rule. They walk with hunched shoulders, their eyes lowered, their bodies pressed together, and quiet, making themselves smaller than they are. I have to become as invisible as can be, S. tells herself She stays as far away from the guards as possible; she thinks that will help her.

The older peasant women do not wash in the courtyard. They carry the water in buckets back to the warehouse and wash themselves there, limb by limb. She is moved by their timidity, even now when they are among other women and when they are reduced to nothing more than a body . . .

It seems to her now as if there was a time when nothing was happening in the camp. It was work, eat, sleep. And it was hot. They stopped expecting that an exchange was imminent, even though such rumours would appear and disquiet them. Exchange had become a remote possibility, a deferred hope. The fact that there was at least a modicum of organisation to life in the camp had a consoling effect, it gave them a sense of certainty and purpose. S. learnt how to break the day up into small fragments which she would then chew, as if they were crumbs of stale bread.

Then one day she sees a group of men right by the woods. It is late, the sun is already setting. The men are digging. But, unlike the women, they are not digging in the field.

Later, while having soup in the kitchen, she recalls the scene of twenty-odd men at the edge of the forest. E. and her daughter Z. are in the kitchen with her. They are meticulously scraping their plates with aluminium spoons. It is a loud sound and it gives S. goose pimples. But they do not often have the opportunity to eat in the kitchen; it is a privilege and they give themselves over to the hot meal, even the little girl looks more cheerful. The soup bowl is on the table with its coat of hard red plastic, and S. takes a second helping. Someone has carved a heart in the plastic with a knife and the sight of it makes her smile. So, somebody was once in love here in this canteen, or maybe simply bored.

The cook, D., has been in the camp for about a month. She used to cook in the men's camp. She blushes whenever she talks, a trait that S. finds appealing. D. sometimes invites them into the kitchen to give them a piece of meat or cake, probably leftovers from the lunch eaten by the camp's administrators. She says she invites them because of the little girl, the child is so skinny, but all three of them eat, little Z. eating the least, without appetite.

S. asks D. about the other camp and the men at the edge of the forest. Is it true that they kill and bury them and then level out the earth with bulldozers? D. shakes her head vaguely, she says that she used to see them herself, digging at the edge of the woods and that it is most certainly not a good sign. Obviously, she does not want to talk in front of the little girl. When she is sure the child is paying no attention, she makes a swift gesture with her hand, as if drawing a knife across her throat.

Sometimes the guards come for E. and she goes off to the administration building or even to the men's camp. She returns sullen and silent. She smokes nervously, taking a few drags and then passing the cigarette on. She looks at no one, avoiding S.'s eye while they work, and to S. it is obvious that E. knows something she does not. She begs E. to tell her. Better not ask, it's better for you not to know, says E. Terrible things are going on there, she says, turning her head away so that the child does not hear.

Others talk, however. The guards themselves, to start with. And the women who have heard it from them and from other women. Stories spread through the camp about torture and about the thousands of people killed in the men's camp. The women say they have heard that prisoners over there have their eyes gouged out, pieces of flesh sliced from their living bodies, their bones broken. S. cannot stand it any more. She begs E. to tell her what she has seen. E. merely confirms that she has seen mutilated corpses.

Two women from their warehouse clean the administration building at the bottom of the courtyard. They tell S. that in one of the rooms they often find blood splattered on the floor and the walls. They wash it off with a spray of water. Then they wipe down the walls with a rag. But they are hard to wash completely clean, says one of them, that would take chlorine or saline acid. The once white walls are now covered with ugly brown, yellow and red stains.

S. does not know what to make of these rumours. She is afraid that people exaggerate and invent the most horrible stories. Shooting people dead and burying their bodies by the woods seems horrible enough to her. She herself has seen people digging what was probably a pit for the corpses. But torture . . .

She is sitting by the open window in the kitchen. Alone. Two guards pass by, she can hear the crunch of their footsteps on the gravel. They are talking. Their voices are carried in uneven gusts by the early evening breeze. There is mention of torture by electricity in the other camp. They apparently saw it with their own eyes and are now talking about it. They utter the words: electric cable, saw. She feels she will lose her mind at the very mention of these words.

How can I ever explain to anybody the isolation we were kept in? Everything got around, but the news was unreliable, unconfirmed. Even though it is happening right next to you, you don't believe it. And even if you do believe it, you cannot dwell on it, it would be the end of you. You believe it only if you yourself see it. Perhaps this deliberate blindness is a form of self-preservation.

The camp, Bosnia

JUNE 1992

One evening, while there is still daylight in the warehouse, she takes her things out of her backpack. She has to prove to herself that she still exists as a person, as S., if only through her belongings. Until that summer her identity had seemed indisputable. She knew who she was, she had family and friends, a job, interests . . . Now, however, she is inhabiting an underground world where the rules are different. She is connected to her previous world by the slim hope that it is still possible to be the same person, but already senses the fragility of this hope, the uncertainty of her own existence. She feels like a cracked bowl which is slowly leaking water. Even her memories are becoming remote and inaccessible.

But her old blue backpack and belongings show her that perhaps this is not so. The little she has from her other life is packed inside it and from time to time S. feels the need to return to herself through these possessions. She takes them out of the backpack and lays them out around her on the blanket: underwear, tops, a sweater, a notebook, pencils, a photo album and a cosmetics bag.

She fingers the little photograph album. She does not open it, not yet. For the time being, it is enough that it is here with her, like a letter of guarantee or a birth certificate.

She has decided that she will open it only in the case of dire necessity, if ever she manages to recognise such necessity. She knows all the photographs by heart anyway, and looking at them would only cause her even more of the pain she knows so well. These pictures are her strongest proof that there truly did exist a person named S., twenty-nine years of age, a graduate of the Teacher Training College, temporarily employed in the village of B. as a home-room teacher, single, 1.68 metres tall, brown hair, brown eyes, no birthmarks . . . Like the man from Grbavica who had lost half his face to cancer of the jaw and who, when she was sitting outside in the summer garden one day, had shown her his photograph. Here, this is me, the man had said, unable to reconcile himself to his disfigured face.

She does not recognise herself in this camp. Who am I, wonders S. as, one by one, she returns her things, her precious belongings, to the backpack. The beautiful soft shoes which still smell new, and the red dress. What is the point of these shoes and the dress, will she ever wear them again? Then she thinks it is a miracle that the backpack and belongings are still with her, that she has not lost them, that they have not stolen them from her.

But something *is* missing. S. rummages nervously through her backpack again, then empties it on to the blanket. She sees that she is missing the little box with her gold jewellery. She feels her lips quiver and is afraid that she will cry, that she will sob like a hurt child. Somebody has stolen her gold neck chain, earrings and locket. How can that be? Did the guards do it, do they go through their things when the women are not in the warehouse? But they have no need to do that. They can order all of them to turn over their remaining gold jewellery, if any of them still has any left. Just the way they did in the bus. First they asked for money. They said give over your money and the women had to give it over. Some of them had no money and gave their gold jewellery instead, their necklaces and rings. Later they asked for articles of gold. The women gave whatever they had left. S. had decided to risk it. First she carried her little jewellery box in her bra, then she returned it to the backpack, certain that the guards now thought they had nothing left.

It is not the loss of the jewellery that upsets her as much as the thought that it might have been taken by one of the women, by one of her fellow prisoners. Why, why? If the women prisoners cannot count on one another, then there is nothing she can trust any more. If the women themselves can steal from each other, then they can inform on each other, perhaps do even worse than that. She does not care about the articles themselves. She even thinks that it may be best to be done with this senseless attachment to things. What upsets her is the feeling of diminishment, impoverishment and effacement. She wonders what else she will have to give up and what is the minimum of things with which one can survive without losing the feeling that one is human?

S. is haunted by this feeling of betrayal for a long time afterwards. It is perfectly clear to her now that she cannot trust anyone. Placing the backpack under her head she knows that she may not find it there again tomorrow. A wall of suspicion is building between her and the women around her in the warehouse. Solitude is pressing in on her. If she survives, she will survive alone, in spite of, rather than together with the other women. She is infuriated by her own stupidity and naivety. Cramped on her patch of blanket, for the first time she feels desolate. She will not believe anyone any more, she will be cautious, she won't help anybody. It exhausts her just to think about everything she would have to do to protect herself against such assaults. Who knows whether she will have the strength to carry all this out?

She dreams that she is eating. There is some sort of celebration, a birthday party perhaps, or a wedding. Sitting around the table are unfamiliar faces. Everyone is dressed up but eating with their hands. S. is amused that they are having trouble eating the roast meat and potatoes with their fingers. Although the waiters notice, they do not bring them any cutlery. Only she has cutlery; she does not think anybody else notices. S. is eating *Wiener schnitzel* and a green salad. The cutlet is enormous and no matter how hard S. tries, its size does not diminish. The fact that the cutlet refuses to disappear gives her immense pleasure, and she licks her lips loudly in her sleep . . .

Sometimes she manages to relax completely. It is then that she imagines being in her room in her parents' flat in Sarajevo; she has not yet gone to work as a substitute teacher in the village school, perhaps she has not yet even finished her studies. She imagines that she is lying on her bed (oh, what she would not give now to fall into that familiar dip in the mattress), leafing through a fashion magazine. Lazily she turns the glossy pages, skimming the article about how to recognise the man for you, the confessions of a famous actress, letters to the editor and vegetarian recipes. The light falls from the little lamp on to the paper, the scent of roses in bloom wafts in from the balcony, the television can be heard through the open door of her room and it merges with the voices coming in off the street. She might be nibbling at an almond and vanilla bun and periodically casting a look at her polished nails, pondering how the red polish has already chipped and it is time to do her nails again, and how this year's fashion has nothing interesting to offer. Doing something ordinary again. Everyday things. Soothed by this unreal picture, she drops off to sleep, remembering the taste of the vanilla in the buns.

A summer storm; the women run in from the field, soaked and breathless. Inside the warehouse, they sit down, listening to the rain pelting on to the thin asbestos roof and for a moment they forget where they are. The storm has cooled the air. Suddenly, it is easier to breath, the air smells of camomile and mint, and of freshly cut grass. You can even smell the concrete in the courtyard. The atmosphere in the warehouse becomes light-hearted, there is an excitement in the air because of the change, like a holiday afternoon. S. feels as if they have stolen this day from the guards and kept it just for themselves . . .

E.'s daughter likes to draw, but it is hard to get hold of paper in the camp. Art used to be Z.'s favourite subject in school. S. gives her her empty notebook and Z. sketches portraits in it, her strokes quick and precise. There is something mature and serious about her drawings—women standing in line for food, a pensive face, the camp. Sometimes S. watches her draw. She is calm and composed when she works, as if what she is doing is terribly important to her. S. is happy for her because she thinks this makes it easier for the girl to bear life in the camp. When she is drawing, Z. is in a world of her own and this soothes her. Only her little, frowning face betrays sadness.

S. does not yet know how important this ordinary notebook with its thin grey covers and drawings inside will become one day. *It is the only proof I have that I was not dreaming, that I was in the camp.*

The main foods in the camp are cabbage and potato soup, margarine, liverwurst, macaroni, peas and rice. Sometimes there is a bit of milk for the children, and marmalade or cookies. The food depends on the delivery, on whether the truck has come in time. What they miss most is bread. The bread in the camp is stale and dry, even mouldy sometimes. The women talk about how to make bread, baklava, pies and different kinds of cakes. Such delicacies are inaccessible to them now. As she listens to the women, S. can smell the meat and the soup, she can almost hear the crunch of the freshly baked bread against her teeth.

She no longer sees the warehouse as a warehouse, but rather as an apartment building where she has a flat—her blanket. Except the apartments are not separated by walls. Private territory is delineated by blankets. The women who know each other from before have placed themselves close to each other and somehow stick together. Two women once got into a physical fight. The tall, strong woman screamed at the younger woman that she had tricked her, but the latter deftly dodged her blows until the tall woman grabbed her by the hair. The guards separated them, smacking everyone out of the way. They had swapped some belongings and then got into a fight because one of them was unhappy with the exchange. There were not many things that could be traded: soap, buttons, needle and thread, food and clothes. Soap was a very important commodity because they washed their clothes themselves, drying them at night on the wire strung out behind the warehouse. Little of their initial solidarity was left now. Like the others, S. had learned with time that to give is to go without yourself.

She still finds unreal the scene of the two women inmates lunging at each other, as if they had forgotten where they were. Maybe they really did forget. Maybe their fight is a sign of humanity, like gossip, theft, friendship, enmity, pettiness and small favours. You cannot think about death all the time, even when you are living in its shadow.

She continues to hear stories about the men in the other camp. Except the numbers keep growing, as if yeast is being added to them. Now they say that thousands have been killed. E. is absolutely categorical on the subject and that is strange. How? When? And all this is happening right here, next to them? E. gives no details, but she mentions these dreadful, huge, incredible numbers. S. wonders how she has come by this information, but E. knows the manager, she is practically an employee at that camp. E. tells her that they do even worse things to the women. There is a room in the administration building that they call the 'women's room'; she says that this is where the youngest and prettiest girls are put. Soldiers from all around visit them at night. As she is talking, E. holds her so tightly by the arm that S. cannot but feel the enormity of her fear.

She has, of course, already heard of the 'women's room' from others. These stories seem far more likely to her than those of torture. Who could stop the guards or soldiers from doing whatever they want with the women? Only the commander of the camp, assuming he has no part in it himself. She had not noticed this sort of lust in the eyes of the young man who had come for her. He probably had not had time to do anything. The buses were waiting, the people had to be assembled in the gym. But in the camp there is time enough. The best thing would be to keep myself invisible, she thinks to herself, curling up on her bedding.

The stories themselves are enough for her to imagine the guard coming for her at night, ordering her to get up and follow him. For a moment she hopes it is a mistake. It is no mistake. She lies there riveted to the floor. She feels so heavy that she cannot get up immediately. Then two guards lift her up and take her away. She stumbles. She shouts. One of them slaps her hard, catching her mouth. She can taste the blood on her lips. She sees that no one can help her; the women cower in fear of being taken away themselves. They are outside the warehouse now. Night has fallen. S. tries to wrestle free of the guards. Their breath reeks of brandy. Her struggling amuses them, they laugh, as if her attempt to break free is the funniest thing in the world. She is as helpless as a child in their grip. But she keeps struggling, as if still hoping to escape . . .

We are all infected by the camp in the same way, she thinks. Of tainted blood, we are all the same. Women exist here only in the plural now. Nameless, faceless, interchangeable. There are only two categories, young and old.

One night she is awoken by a commotion, footsteps and muffled cries at the other end of the warehouse. It all happens quickly and in pitch darkness. There is just the gleam of the flashlight slicing through the dark like a sword. Quiet, the guard yells angrily, quiet! It is utterly unnecessary, because he is the only one making any noise. Her first thought is to look for E. She gets up, but somebody grabs her by the arm and pulls her back down. She lies there paralysed with fear. She does not dare ask what is happening, she can only guess. Then she decides that she does not really want to know, that the sudden commotion does not concern her. After a while she falls asleep again, as if nothing had happened.

The next morning the other women confirm what she has already guessed about the nocturnal incident. The guards had come for the girls. They must have seen them before, because they knew exactly who they were looking for. They observed them during the day, while they were working, eating, resting, that was when the victims were chosen. Then last night they had walked among the sleeping women, flashlights illuminating faces, until they found those two particular girls.

The girls are not back yet. S.'s hope that she will not meet the same fate slowly fades, but she cannot let go of her belief that something will save her.

In the following few days there is much to do for a child who has a temperature and diarrhoea. S. does not find it hard to work, it stops her from thinking about recent events.

The girls have still not come back and an unusual silence has been cast over the women for days now. As darkness descends, so does the dread. The silence. The anticipation. Listening for the footsteps, for the shouting of the guards. The fear of men, of what they can do to women. The first to speak in the dark is V. She stutters at first, as if choking on the rush of words because she can no longer contain this tangible, suffocating fear, hers and theirs. Then she slows down and lowers her voice, half-whispering to no one in particular. Her words shatter the silence in which each of the women has only one single thought on her mind.

V. says that it has already happened to her, when the soldiers came to her village, led her husband away and locked her up in the bedroom. There were several of them. They did it to me on my own marital bed, she says, that was the worst thing. No, she had felt no pain, nothing, absolutely nothing at all. She had been completely without feeling, like a log of wood. She cannot say how long it lasted or how many soldiers there were. One hurried up the other, the sound of gunfire and pandemonium could be heard outside. She did not resist them. The last one told her, you were as quiet as a lamb. Perhaps that is why they let her live, even though it would have been better if they hadn't, she says.

When they left, she remained there on the bed. She lay there and felt as if she were dying, she felt herself die piece by piece, exactly that, piece by piece. Her hands. Her legs. Her heart. She did not think of death, she simply knew that what was happening to her right then was her death. If it had not been for the children I would have let them kill me, she says. Her life ended there, on her marital bed.

K. sits next to her, trembling. Her shoulders are shaking as if it was all happening to her. She cannot be much older than S. Her face is rugged from working outside in the field. S. holds her hand.

She had come to the camp alone, but S. knows that she had two children. K. says nothing, but the trembling increases. Something worse than rape must have happened to this woman, something unspeakable. But K. cannot talk about what happened to her children.

The other women start talking about their experiences now. S. senses that they are doing so for the first time, the words barely cross their lips. Somebody lights a candle and the weak flame flickers on the warehouse walls.

S. cannot see their faces as they talk, she sees merely distorted shadows and hears their voices in the semi-darkness. Somewhere at the other end of the room a woman says: they defiled my daughter in front of my eyes. They made me watch. I offered them German marks. They took the money. I offered them my gold jewellery, just to leave her alone. They took the jewellery but they did not leave her alone. It lasted all day. In the end they . . . killed her. Then S. hears another, very young voice near the door, like an echo of the first: I was going down through the woods to the neighbouring village. I saw three dead girls in a ditch. I knew them from school. They were naked. Their breasts had been cut off. I covered them with leaves.

The voice belonging to the little girl says they did it to her older sister. She watched from her hiding place in the attic. Her sister screamed but a soldier clamped his hand down over her mouth. Then she saw her sister run naked into the woods. They never found her. Her mother said that maybe she is still alive, she is sure that she is still alive.

They fall silent again. Well, you can survive anything, adds the first woman, as if to excuse the fact that she is still alive and in their midst.

How is it possible to survive all that? S. senses that here the survival instinct is the highest law of existence. She is not ready to acquiesce to that, not yet. The words *you can survive anything* reflect a state of awareness she is still unable to fathom. Perhaps it has an encouraging effect on all of them living in the camp, because they believe that this too they will survive. She herself does not know where she is, sitting among unknown peasant women on a muggy summer evening and accepting her fate. The fact that she is a city girl and that she is educated is of no help to her here, not in this situation. What makes her any different from the woman who said you can survive anything, S. wonders? Only that she refuses to accept it, that this childish, deliberate dissociation from reality is her way of sparing herself.

That was the only time she heard the women talk about rape. They did not talk about it later, they did not mention it again. If word got around that they had been defiled they would not be able to go back home to their villages, their husbands or parents. So they hold their tongues, they really believe they will go back home, S. thinks to herself. *It must have been so hard for them to live with such a burden, with that kind of fear.*

She thinks she can tell which women it happened to by how they suddenly fall silent if the subject should happen to arise, or avert their eyes from the person talking. Their careful skirting of the subject, their avoidance of certain words, their look, betrays them . . . the secret signs of what they so wrongly call their 'disgrace'.

One morning before the women set out to work in the field, five girls are pulled aside. They have not done this openly, in broad daylight, until now. The women stand in total silence, as if struck dumb, until dislodged from their place by a flurry of blows. The girls stand a bit further away, in the courtyard, pressed against each other. One of them is terribly young, she cannot be more than thirteen years old. S. knows her, she comes from the next village. A. has a bandage on her hand, one that S. had recently put on because A. had hurt her finger. Standing in the sunlight with her head bowed, her black hair glows as if on fire.

The guard says he is taking them to the administration building for questioning, as if in this camp they ever question the women. He is a short, bearded man, dressed in a dirty t-shirt, with huge stains of perspiration under his arms. He tosses out these words to the others with a wink, as if it is a good joke.

It is an oppressive day, or at least so it seems to S. She watches them walk toward the building. The girls hold on to each other, stumbling as if slightly dazed by the sun. They look back towards the warehouse, but no one there can help them. At one moment A. turns around and waves at S. with her injured hand. It is an uncertain, timid gesture. Then her hand falls limply by her side. I will never see her again, S. thinks to herself, shivering as if an icy wind has grazed her skin. By the time she summons the strength to lift her arm and wave back, A. is already far away, at the other end of the courtyard. She does not turn around and S. feels the futility of her gesture.

There is a stickiness to time that day, it drags slowly. A soldier walks into the warehouse in the early afternoon. She first sees him standing in the doorway, sees only his black outline, a dark shadow blocking the only source of light in the warehouse. The soldiers sometimes come by during the day looking for E. She usually goes with them either to the men's camp or to the administration building to treat one of their people. They would usually call out to her from the courtyard because they did not feel like walking all the way to the warehouse in the heat. Now this man is standing in the doorway. He does not move. He is waiting. He is waiting for his eyes to adjust to the semi-darkness. *Ti!* You, he shouts, you! Over here! S. thinks how stupid his order sounds without a verb. E. gets up, takes her doctor's bag and heads toward him. Not you, her! He can only mean S. because apart from the sick woman, she is the only other person in the warehouse at that moment.

E. persists. She walks over and tries to explain something to him. She tells him that she is a nurse, that she is the one they probably need, not S., it is a mistake, it is she they always call to the administration building. Her words ricochet off the soldier as if he was made of steel. Wordlessly, he pushes her aside. Just as he makes no effort to use verbs, he makes no move to go and get S. He simply extends his hand. Or a finger, straight and ominous. And that pronoun, spoken in the tone of a command. *Ti*. You. He stands there blocking out the sun. Waiting.

S. wipes her hands on her skirt, the way housewives do when someone catches them in the middle of making lunch. Or like very old women who wipe their hands on their aprons before shaking hands with an unknown visitor who finds them at the stove. Her hands are clammy. All she can feel are the palms of her hands and her throat. Suddenly she cannot swallow her own saliva.

Finally, S. takes a step. She walks towards that shadow at the other end of the warehouse. She remembers him as being huge. She walks, her throat dry, unaware of her automatic movements. Her legs carry her in spite of her will, as if they have a life of their own. She can hear her steps echoing strangely against the concrete floor, as if they are not hers. She thinks she hears somebody crying. The wings of a bird flutter under the warehouse roof. As she walks by, she sees E.'s white face and fixed stare. She thinks she has never seen such big eyes before.

She walks very slowly, at least it seems so to her. Her head is a void. She feels pressure in her temples and in her chest. And a kind of tautness, as if her veins will burst and her blood spill out. She will collapse dead, right here in the middle of the warehouse.

Then she sees his face, close up. His skin is young and tight. His eyes are dark and completely opaque. There is no expression on this face, no grimace. He says not a word. He just watches, gravely. He searches her face. His eyes slide down to her breasts and then lower still.

S. remembers his hot, searching male stare as they walk together across the courtyard.

She has that same feeling of surprise and immobility that she had that morning when the young man burst into her kitchen. Suddenly her body feels so heavy that she can hardly budge. Her movements are sluggish and hesitant, her brain is drained. She wants to scream. To shout. But her mouth is dry, not a single word finds its way through her constricted throat. She wants to run away; she really would run if only she could step away, if only she had the will to do so. S. notices that she no longer has a will of her own, it has been replaced by something else, as if a robot has taken control of her body, making it move and react in her stead. Again, it is happening to someone else and to her at the same time.

It seems a long and tiring way from the warehouse to the building at the end of the courtyard. With the sun behind her, S. can now see her shadow stretch out before her, first over the concrete and then over the gravel. As his boots crunch the gravel, the soldier's shadow overtakes hers.

They stand in front of the door. The soldier kicks it open. They enter a room, an office. The linoleum on the floor is torn and tatty. A cheap office desk stands in the middle of the room. The walls are painted to the halfway mark in a shiny grey. One man is seated, two are standing. They are soldiers, dressed in camouflage uniforms with some sort of insignia sewn on to their sleeves and epaulettes. The window is closed, the air full of cigarette smoke. All three men are smoking and S. thinks to herself how they must be sweltering in those uniforms. The tall soldier who brought her in departs, closing the door behind him.

A man with beady little eyes walks up to her. He looks dangerous. He removes the belt from his trousers. He is going to hit me, I know he is going to hit me, S. thinks to herself feverishly, shutting her eyes in anticipation of the blow. She raises her arms in self-defence. But nothing happens. Another man, the one sitting down, gets up and removes his belt as well. S. is still holding her arms up over her face, but he does not hit her either. The two men stand there holding their belts in their hands and then the tallest of the three walks up to her. He tells her to undress.

S. tries to unbutton her blouse. Three pairs of men's eyes watch her movements as her trembling fingers fail to find the buttons. It is not that she does not want to obey their order. On the contrary, she is in a hurry to do so. At that moment she cannot even think about doing anything else, there is no chance of her not obeying them. As she stands there unbuttoning her top, her intention must be clear to them, but S. no longer controls her fingers. She is betrayed by her hands which lack the strength even for such a small, simple movement.

Then one of them loses patience. With a practised hand he pulls out a knife and presses it against her throat. Hurry up, he hisses through clenched teeth, hurry up! At that same instant she is again struck by their inability to express themselves in normal sentences; they use only monosyllabic words, as if they have forgotten how to speak. *And perhaps they have. Perhaps that happens to people in wartime, words suddenly become superfluous because they can no longer express reality. Reality escapes the words we know, and we simply lack new words to encapsulate this new experience.*

A second soldier is not so 'gentle'. He neither threatens nor speaks, he simply walks up to her and rips her blouse off.

Now she is standing naked in the office, leaning against the wall. She is surrounded by hunters. Their eyes are on her breasts. She can feel them crawl all over her. They are wet, slimy, hot, as they climb her neck, as they touch her nipples and descend over her belly to her loins. This is perhaps the worst thing that will engrave itself on her memory: the eyes of strange men revelling in their trophy just before the moment of attack. She knows they are going to attack her. She knows she has been caught in a trap like a wild beast, and there is no escape. The pounding of her heart drowns out all sound. The cigarette smoke stings her eyes. Tears shut out their faces like a curtain.

She does not know how long she has been standing there, leaning against the wall. Finally, two of them take her to the desk. They tie her arms and legs with their belts. She resists only briefly. In a last, vain attempt to break free, her body arches instinctively, and then suddenly falls limp, as if dead.

When the first of the three men penetrates her, S. feels momentary pain. Later she feels nothing more than a thrust, which pushes the desk ever closer to the window. She turns her head to the wall. A greenbottle fly paces up and down the wall nervously, as if it has lost something. Finally it has found that something. For a long time it stands still, rubbing its legs together. Then it flies up to the ceiling. S. follows it with her eyes. And at that moment she sees her own legs and a man's head poking out between them. The man has his eyes closed and mouth open.

She looks for the fly again. Now it is sitting on the light bulb. The bulb is slowly swaying. When she looks down, she sees that her legs are still there but now another man's head is between them. These are her legs, of course. S. tells herself that these are her legs, but she does not actually feel them. As if I am not here, she thinks. As if I am gone. All she can feel is the hard surface of the table under her back as it inches closer and closer to the window. She can already see the courtyard through the dirty windowpane and several guards relaxing by the fence. It is a lovely sunny day. A summer afternoon.

Their grunting fills the small room. Perhaps they are even saying something. Cursing, yes, they are cursing her mother. One of them is trying to look into her face. He turns her face his way, yelling that she will remember him, that she has to remember him. He reeks. Yes, she will remember his breath, that she will remember. But not his face. His face blurs with the ceiling and with the fly, which is still idly swinging on the light bulb.

The legs of the desk keep sliding across the linoleum from his rough thrusting. The wooden desk creaks. If only that creaking would stop, and that groaning and panting, that noise which rises over her and covers her like a lid.

S. feels no pain. Something inside her has snapped in two. She is completely at peace, completely outside herself. She is lying on the floor. Her hands are untied. Her lips sting. She touches them. There is a faint trace of blood on her fingers. She still does not fully feel her body, merely this cut on her lip which stings ferociously.

Then there is the boot on her chest. The dull pain forces the breath from her lungs. Open your mouth, says a man's voice. He is standing over her, his legs spread. Open your mouth! S. opens her mouth. There is a long stream of urine. Swallow, he orders, I'll teach you obedience. She tries to swallow. The urine is warm and salty and makes her want to vomit. She coughs and throws up at the same time. He slaps her. Now she swallows it as obediently as a child but he keeps on hitting her as if this gives him particular pleasure. He hits her with the flat of his hand. He hits hard and her head reels from one side to the other but still nothing hurts. By now it is all the same to her, whatever he does.

Being hit is the last thing she remembers, how one of the soldiers keeps slapping her again and again and again. Then she loses consciousness.

The 'women's room', Bosnia

JUNE–JULY 1992

S. comes to. She opens her eyes. The first thing she sees are the tablecloths hanging over the window, and slats of wood nailed across them. The sun is shining directly on to the two windows at the back of the room and penetrating the red and white checks, creating a colourful pattern on the floor beside her. This must have been an office before. Now mattresses and blankets have been thrown on to the bare floor. Two girls are sleeping in each other's arms on the next mattress.

She does not know when she was brought into this room. All she remembers is shivering with a fever and somebody covering her gently. A hand lifts her head into a lap. Drink, she hears a woman's voice say, you have to drink. She can still taste the blood in her mouth. She takes a few sips of cold water. Then her head drops to the side again.

Later the other girls tell her that she remained in this feverish state for several days. E. came and gave her some medicine. Pain-killers probably. She was worried. She was afraid there might be internal bleeding, it had already happened once. The girl had died of sepsis. S. was unconscious for three days. Her body simply coped with the temperature on its own. The girls changed the cold compresses on her forehead and brought her tea. She remembers nothing.

Finally her temperature dropped, she came to. She had a cut on the inside of her lip and her face was swollen from being battered. Every inch of her body hurt; she still felt pain in her womb, like a burning sensation, pain in her wrists and pain in her back and muscles which made it hard for her to move on the mattress. During those few days and nights, pain had moved into S. as if into its own house. She felt occupied. A previously unknown illness had entered her and was now eating away at her. S. could not imagine that a man's body could do such damage to a woman, that it was so powerful, so unfairly overpowering that a woman had no defence against such force.

She does not feel whole any more. She cannot explain this feeling to herself. It is not as if she is missing a part of her body, an arm or a leg. On the contrary, they say that people who have had a limb amputated feel that limb for a long time afterwards, as if it was still there, still alive. S. lies there with her eyes closed. Daylight penetrates her closed eyelids and a soft purple light illuminates her darkness. She feels as if she is trying to see herself from inside, to convince herself that she is still whole. All she can see is this blood-red darkness, the circulation of her own blood and the flickering particles of light in the throbbing of her pulse.

More clearly than ever before she feels stripped of her right to herself, completely dispossessed of her own body.

Leaning against the cold wall, S. takes stock of her new prison. A rope is strung across the middle of the room. Laundry is hanging from it: bras, panties, hankies and a blue blouse. The room is so small that you can only lie down or sit on the mattresses or on the floor. It is muggy. There are nine of them in the room. She inhales the faint smell of old mattresses and women perspiring.

Still, she consoles herself that at least some sort of order exists here. The blankets are neatly folded, the mattresses placed in a circle to leave at least a bit of free space in the middle. The shoes are lined up in a corner by the door: white summer sandals with worn heels, canvas slippers, a few pairs of sneakers. And a pair of black high-heel shoes. Whose shoes are those, she wonders, shoes that belong to another world and that arouse a sadness in her. She thinks of the hope that this pair of shoes exudes, and of her Italian shoes in her back-pack. Like S., this girl had at one moment thought that such a pair of shoes might come in handy wherever the orange bus was taking her. She could not part with them. Perhaps she had been wearing them at the time. S. wants to tell them something about how stupidly naive all this is, but her head is spinning.

The girls are asleep or dozing. One is humming a song, another is by the window reading a tattered novel. Her neighbour on the mattress is M., one of the girls recently taken away from the warehouse. She tells S. that this is that 'women's room'. The one E. had mentioned to her. Why hadn't she told her what it looks like? She was bound to know, she drops by here, S. thinks to herself bitterly. Maybe she thought S. would avoid winding up here. The door to the corridor is locked. The key is with the wife of the former warehouse janitor, who brings them food. Except for the soldiers and the guards, N. is the only other person the girls see. They tell S. that she is good to them.

The other door, the door to the toilet, is unlocked. We have our own toilet and sink, says M., with a dose of pride. She tells her what S. herself has already guessed, that the women locked up here are at the disposal of the soldiers, who come at will, usually at night. Sometimes they pick them and sometimes they don't. Some girls never return to the 'women's room'. M. writes down the dates in a little notebook, then crosses them out. She is afraid she would go crazy otherwise.

While she was in the warehouse S. feared uncertainty. Any kind of certainty seemed preferable to her. Now she was at least rid of that fear. There was no more uncertainty. She was in a storehouse of women, in a room where female bodies were stored for the use of men.

The girls actually do have their own toilet, a real toilet, one for the nine of them, a luxury. It has a door which can be closed but not locked. And a white ceramic sink, albeit cracked. Cold tap water. The hot water tap can also be turned on, but it releases only air. Cold water does not bother her, it is summer anyway. *At the time I was still hoping that winter would not find me in the same place.*

She sees an elongated bar of pink soap on the edge of the sink. It smells of lilies. She is not sure whether it is allowed, but she cannot resist the temptation of washing herself and she reaches for the soap. First she washes her face and neck, then her breasts, under her arms and between her legs. What a wonderful, precious thing soap is. In the toilet, behind the closed door, S. happily inhales the fresh scent.

The toilet walls are covered in green tiles and the place is big enough to hold a metal basin and jug as well as the toilet bowl and sink. One of the girls is soaking her underwear, planning to wash it later. To S., the basin is like a godsend. She will be able to shower and wash her hair in peace and quiet, but she decides to put it off until later. She still feels weak. The pain in her stomach has passed, but she has huge, sore bruises on her face and breasts.

The room also has a small window which is not nailed up with boards; it does not even have bars because it is so small that no one could squeeze through it. When she stands on the toilet bowl, which has no lid, she can see the courtyard which must be behind the administration building. The courtyard is completely empty, discounting the three huge rusty Dumpsters. Behind the barbed wire fence are the woods, a lovely pinewood forest. S. drinks in the cold wet smell and it restores her strength. I'm alive, she thinks, as if this were a secret to be kept to herself. Rising above the dark green trees is the blue of the summer sky. Cobalt blue, like in her pupils' drawings.

The mirror is gone, although you can clearly see where it once hung over the sink. Perhaps it is better this way, perhaps it is better for her not to see herself, not now. If you look in the mirror over the sink every day you think you are seeing yourself and the reflection gives you a certain sense of security, of self-confidence. But there is no point in looking at your own face unless you can actually recognise it. S. does not want to recognise herself. None of them want to recognise themselves in the captivity of the 'women's room'. They are now different people and their faces are no longer their own, they belong to the camp.

At that moment in that room she realises that the camp is not just a place where she happens to find herself, it has become the condition of her body and soul.

During the day, the 'women's room' is shrouded in semi-darkness; streaks of sun penetrate the cracks in the boards, creating dazzling patterns on the floor. Sounds waft in from the courtyard—men's voices, indistinct orders, shouts, the tramping of many feet, murmuring and cries. No one in the room pays any attention, or so it seems to S. M. turns on to her side, curling up into an even tighter ball. No one goes near the window, not even to try and peek through the cracks to see what is going on outside. Or do these residents of the 'women's room' perhaps know something that S. does not yet know? They do not go to the window, they are not interested in what is happening to others, as if they are prisoners of a separate reality which has laws and rules of its own. For them the murmuring and voices outside can mean only more soldiers and guards who will appear at their door at night, drunk, dirty and dangerous. That is a moment to be postponed, they do not want to think about what is unavoidable anyway. They are upset only by footsteps in the corridor. Then they quickly try to guess whether they are N.'s footsteps in slippers, or the heavy footsteps of men. How many are there? One or more? Soldiers or guards? All this needs to be urgently deciphered the moment the shuffle of feet can be heard at the end of the corridor.

Despite the heat, the girls lie down dressed. As if not one of them wishes to display her naked body. Nakedness reminds them of what they do not want to contemplate, of violence. The body has to be concealed as much as possible, made as invisible, as undesirable as possible. They cannot hide from the men at whose disposal they lie. Here women no longer have the right to say no. They hide from themselves, cover themselves up with clothes which in men's hands turn instantly into rags and tatters.

S. no longer knows whether the girls around her are pretty and attractive; these words lose the meaning they have in normal life. Like her, the others seem to have lost a sense of their appearance. In the 'women's room' remembrance of the world outside is reflected in washed clothes, neatly folded articles and the floral scent of soap on their skin.

M., the girl with whom she shares the mattress, can smell the soap on S.'s skin. You don't have to save on soap, she says, it belongs to everyone. S. finds it strange that no one here saves on soap. M. laughs. Oh, we have been known to get shampoo sometimes too, and cookies and cheese, she says. From the soldiers? No, from the woman who watches us.

Dinner arrives. It is a pot of soup. N. brings it in. She was living here before, her husband was the watchman at the warehouse. She is tasked with overseeing the 'women's room'. The strands of grey hair escaping from under the kerchief on her head and the deep lines in her fair skin make S. think that she must be old. But it is hard to say how old. She is toothless, and that makes her nose and chin jut out. She is wearing a kind of indeterminate greyish-brown apron. On her feet, despite the summer, she has socks made of homespun wool. She looks menacing to S. Bean soup again? We had that yesterday, says K. She speaks without a hint of accusation or even surprise, but sadly somehow. S. thinks the old woman may slap her. But she merely gives a dismissive wave of her hand and a toothless smile. Her face is transformed by the smile and suddenly she looks terribly kind.

The truck didn't arrive, she mumbles, spreading her arms helplessly. I'm eating beans the same as you girls, she says as if to justify herself. When the truck does not show up it means that you eat what there is, old tins of beans, rotting potatoes that taste sweet, cabbage. For some reason there is never a shortage of cabbage. And so it continues until the truck arrives from B., and that depends on whether there is fighting in the area or not. Sometimes N. goes to the next village, about a two-hour walk from the camp, brings back a chicken for her husband and herself, and makes chicken soup for the girls. Plain, thin and watery, its taste is nonetheless reminiscent of home-made soup.

S. does not remember the day, but she does remember the moment that N. took out of her apron a round golden loaf of bread, corn bread. It was still warm. J. grabbed the bread from her hands and kissed it. She carried it around the room, holding it out for each girl to smell. For S. there was nothing more wonderful than the smell of freshly baked bread, of buns which her mother would bring back from the corner bakery in the morning, before S. and her sister were up. When she opened the front door the smell would fill the entire apartment. They would wake up and find waiting on the table for them the bread and the buns, still warm and fragrant.

N. breaks up the bread and suddenly they feel as if there is no war and they are not in a camp. N. sits down with the girls. She does not eat, she merely observes their delight over the fresh bread she has just baked for them, for these women abandoned by God. Theirs and everyone else's. Eat, children, she says, bread will give you the strength to go on. You've got to have strength. These horrors will pass. The youngest of the girls, A., swallows her morsels as if they are about to be stolen from her. Later she has a stomach ache.

N. brings them breakfast, lunch and dinner and tries to get them some fruit or cookies or a package of cream cheese. They sweep the room themselves, and she sometimes washes their towels for them. She brings them soap and shampoo, sometimes an article of clothing. Shoes. A skirt. Whose clothes are they? Where is the woman they belonged to, what has happened to her? Is she dead? Was she killed? No one dares ask where N. gets all these things, whether she takes them from other women to give to the girls in the room. These articles are all too valuable. S. is certain that she does not want to know too much, nothing that would add to the burden or raise her suspicions about the provenance of these things. It is easier not to think, none of them has the power to change anything anyway. The girls avoid talking about it.

Once N. brought in some coffee and made it in the middle of the room, on an electric stove she had brought with her. They sat down in a circle, drank the coffee from little cups and nibbled on the sugar cubes. Then she spread a sheet of newspaper out on the floor and the girls placed their cups upside down on it. They waited for N. to read their fortunes in the cups. I see a road, she told A., a long, wide road, as if you're flying. Yes, yes, I see, you have wings, you are flying somewhere. That's good, very good. A. laughs and glides around the room, spreading her arms out like wings. N. sees only good things in the dregs of their coffee cups. She tells J. that she will marry a rich man, H. that she will graduate from the very best schools and V. that she will have lots of children. Their roads are all open and there are lots of letters bearing good news about their families, even though some of their relatives have long since died. They laugh at her inventions, like schoolgirls during recess.

N.'s husband, who guards them, never enters the room. He ordered the window boarded up because the windows on the first floor of the administration building have no bars. As if anyone could escape that way without breaking a leg. Sweetie, the window is too high to make an escape and too low for suicide, H. says solemnly, as if she has already seriously considered both possibilities. She is the oldest among us. She is tall and loud. She says 'sweetie' to everybody and sometimes she sings songs that bring tears to S.'s eyes.

The boarded-up window makes the room stuffy and the air heavy. The women move sluggishly and are constantly sleepy. Through the cracks they can see the entrance to the building and if the boards were not there they would be able to lean out the window and watch the comings and goings in the courtyard. They can only go out into the back yard, and even then only as a group. N.'s husband stands by with his rifle cocked while they shuffle around the yard, not knowing what to do with themselves. Move away from the fence, he shouts. Move! Move! Yet the barbed wire fence is too high to jump. Anyway, they are too weak from lying around all the time and too dazed by the stuffy air and heat to care about anything, let alone about jumping. What S. remembers of these occasional strolls is the heat of the afternoon and the sun on her skin, the air quivering above the ground and the dull crunch of gravel under their feet. And that harsh voice.

When she was at the warehouse, S. rested at night. After coming in from the field and having their dinner, the women would sit around and talk. The days were long and it did not get dark until quite late. One of the women even had a candle. They would do their washing. They could move about freely in the warehouse's courtyard. At nine o'clock the guard would shout: bedtime! They would go back inside the warehouse, but even then they would not go to sleep right away, they would whisper long into the night.

The residents of the 'women's room' have to learn that for them there are no clearly defined borders between day and night. The girls sleep or nap by day. At night the fear in the room is tangible. As darkness falls they start listening and trying to discern. They hear from afar the arriving cars or trucks. And voices. Then footsteps. They try to guess how many soldiers there are and if they are already drunk. They come almost every night. From nearby combat positions, they say, but who knows whether that is the truth, whether there are any such positions nearby. Sometimes they also come in the daytime, upsetting their fragile routine.

There is no order to their visits, there is nowhere to run or hide. There are only nine girls and every night one of them might be up to 'entertain' one or more times. Illness is no excuse, better not to mention any kind of sickness, as if that would stop them at anything. When night falls, each of the girls has the same thought: is it my turn tonight?

Footsteps in the corridor, getting closer and closer. The door opens. Always abruptly, open wide, as if there is no door knob. They are in the corridor. You would think that the young men would stop to look at what is on offer. Like in a brothel, because this is nothing other than a soldiers' brothel. But most often they act as if it is all the same to them whom they get. They are usually drunk. Perhaps it really is more or less all the same to them. Perhaps that is the point, that it has to be all the same to them. The same wrong blood flows inside each of the women. The differences between them must be so small that the men can easily forget them. They see them as replaceable, which humiliates them even more. *Perhaps it is like that in real life too, perhaps we are far more similar to them than we think, we just don't notice it.*

The moment the armed men appeared in their village, each one of them had ceased to be a person. Now they are even less so, they have been reduced to a collection of similar beings of the female gender, of the same blood. Blood alone is important, the right blood of the soldiers versus the wrong blood of the women.

But the soldiers are no longer people either, except they are less aware of it. For the girls they have become simply dangerous envoys of a supra-personal power which is forcing them to do what they are doing to the women. S. realises that they too are prisoners without any individuality, without a face. Their bodies, their willpower belongs to somebody else—to the army, to the leader, to the nation. They obey and execute the orders of people in whom they believe or are afraid of. For a moment, standing there at the doorstep of the 'women's room', they believe that they are something else. The masters. Do they know that they cannot run away from the war, that they cannot hide, that they too can be killed, S. wonders as she listens out for their footsteps.

One of S.'s nocturnal visitors reminds her of the young man who came for her in her apartment that morning, which now seems so long ago. There is a brusque resolve about him stemming from insecurity as he beckons to her without hesitation, as if he knows that she is the one he wants. S. does not think it was her face or anything about her that drew his attention. She thinks he did not even glance at her but rather pointed at her quite by chance.

He is drunk, and that is usually a bad sign. When they are drunk and in a group, they can be dangerous. Then they invent cruel games for the girls. The idea is to think up ways to cause them the maximum pain. Sometimes the woman cannot endure it. It cannot be said that they kill her deliberately, killing is easy for them. What is hard is to think up a way to humiliate the woman completely.

The young man, a mere child really, is not rough. He holds her hand and, as if in school, they walk down the long corridor to a room. Two soldiers are in the room. Show her what it means to be a man, they crack, throwing him a look. The young man blushes, perhaps he is afraid that the other two will remain in the room with him. But they leave. S. notices his relief. He does not undress, that is taken by visitors to the 'women's room' as a sign of weakness. He simply unzips his fly and throws himself on to the mattress next to S. Where're you from, S. asks him. From N., he says. That's far away, very far, says S., I was there once. He looks at her. She has the impression that more than anything else he wishes he could just pick himself up, go straight home to his far away little town, flop down on his bed, go to sleep and forget everything. The next day his mother would wake him up, make him a strong cup of coffee and everything would be as it once was. They rounded us up, we had to go, he says, as if the terse words explain it all, the cause of the war, the fact that no one has ever asked him a thing, and that he is lying here next to S., an imprisoned woman who serves for entertainment, in some sort of camp in Bosnia. The tone of his voice is almost weepy.

He tries to take her clothes off. His hands are large and clumsy. It does not occur to him to order her to undress; his thick fingers simply get caught up in undoing her skirt. He hesitates, then he gives up. S. does not move. She does not want to make his work any easier for him, that is not for her to do. For the time being, she is glad that he is not rough and that he does not tear at her clothes or slap her. In situations like this, they sometimes slap you, especially if there is more than one of them. But he lays his head upon her breast and falls asleep. S. too dozes off. She knows that all such encounters are a game of chance, and this one looks to her like a win.

But it should not have happened. She should not have let her guard down. Both of them must have fallen asleep. Suddenly someone is banging on the door. The young man leaps to his feet, still dazed with sleep, afraid that someone might catch him in such a humiliating position, that of a child. The other soldier strides in, pushes the kid outside, and remains with S. He wastes neither time nor words. His actions are rough. Whore, whore, whore, he shouts at her. She tries to remain calm, not to react to his words or movements. She lies there voiceless, her eyes shut, like a still warm corpse. For a moment she thinks that she may get through this, that he will not go beyond the usual roughness.

He is done, on his feet already, he takes a few steps and lights a cigarette. Now he will open the door and walk out and she will breathe a sigh of relief, perhaps that will be it for tonight, perhaps the third soldier will not appear, the night is almost over anyway. Her muscles start relaxing, she breathes deeply, she is already elsewhere, outside of this room . . .

The pain is sudden and piercing, like the stab of a knife. Without thinking, she bends her legs and kicks him in the stomach as hard as she can. He falls over, and the thud of his heavy body on the floor reverberates around the room. I'll kill you, I'll kill you, he howls. The other two are already there, holding S. down on the mattress. She cannot budge. She is now completely in their power. She waits, frozen with fear. They are going to kill her, that much is obvious. Then she hears the voice of the watchman. You're not going to kill anybody, he says, go get your kicks with the women prisoners, these girls here are under my protection. Amazingly, the soldier lets her go. He leaves without a word.

N. immediately brings a compress and folds it over S.'s wound. As S. talks about what happened, V. bares her own breasts. They are studded with still fresh cigarette burns. I begged them not to do it to me, but they laughed, she says. The more I cried, the more they laughed. In the end I fainted. S. knows that V. is telling her all this to try to console her somehow, to show her that she did not fare so badly with just one burn on the inside of her thigh. And compared with V.'s round cigarette burns, S.'s mark hardly counts.

She was lucky. What happened to V. could have happened to her; she was that close to really being done for. Actually, looking at V.'s breasts does give her some comfort after all. She sees now that she could have fared even worse.

The other girls heard the soldier bellow that he would kill her. Petrified, they waited for the sound of a gunshot. Later S. confesses that she had hit him. She tells them she hit him so hard that he fell to the floor and that that had infuriated him. Fortunately for her, the watchman rushed in.

They do not believe that she dared to hit a soldier. She sees they are terrified. You shouldn't have done that, M. says darkly. Now they will take it out on us. S. tries to justify herself, she says she was not thinking, she did it instinctively, like an animal defending itself. But you should have thought, J. snaps back at her, the way someone knocking down a stubborn, irrational creature would do. S. sometimes forgets that there is no real solidarity here, merely the struggle for bare existence. Every night they breathe the same fear together. Yet each fears only for herself. S. had committed an offence. Her conduct had placed the girls in danger. The fact that she had placed herself in danger as well, that was her problem. *They were right, of course.*

A. is the youngest in the 'women's room'. She claims to be over fifteen, though it is evident to everyone that she is barely thirteen. Perhaps she thinks that she will fare better like this, or that what is happening to her will be less terrible than it would be for a thirteen-year-old girl. This way she imagines herself as an adult already. She is right. The war has turned her into a woman. Suddenly, overnight, the soldiers made a woman out of this little girl. Her body, still unfamiliar to her, is now even more so.

A. has the clear white skin of a child, and whenever any of the women suddenly addresses her she blushes, the pink blotches staining her face for a long time afterwards. She is frail in build, still undeveloped, weak, as her peasant neighbours would say. It is strange that she should find herself in this room, among these robust village girls with their strong thighs and big breasts. Her breasts are only just beginning to grow, and were it not for her long hair she could still pass for a boy. At first S. did not know how A. had managed to wind up in this room, whether she had caught somebody's eye or it had been pure chance that this unripe creature had been picked for entertainment. Then M. explained that A. had not wanted to be separated from her cousin and so had come voluntarily when the cousin was brought here. She did not really understand what awaited her. She thought she would help the girls, do their washing and the like. But the soldiers grabbed her the very first evening. They savagely raped her, as if taking their revenge for her not being 'the real thing', for having this miserable scrawny kid landed on them.

A. quickly realised that she could do nothing to defend herself against them and at nightfall, she, like her cousin and the other girls, quietly went off with the soldiers and fulfilled their wishes. She became used to them and to life in the room. She had no one left but the girls in the room, they had become her family. This changed only with the disappearance of her cousin who was barely a year older than she. T. simply never returned to the room.

A. has been distraught ever since, as if her only connection with reality has now been broken. If only I knew what happened to her, she says, it would be easier if I knew she was dead. The others think it is better that she does not know. They spare her as much as they can; she is, after all, still only a child. They know that T. is dead and they know how she died: she was strangled. They cannot tell her that because there is no point relating all the things the soldiers did to her cousin before she died. But they cannot lie to her either. She has got to learn that every absence from the 'women's room' means only one thing, death. They console her with the usual stories, that they do not know what happened, maybe T. even managed to escape. This is not the right way, it upsets A. even more, she tells them again that T. would never leave her.

She is inconsolable for a while, then she seems to have made her peace with T.'s disappearance and stops mentioning it. She is different. Her mind is obviously elsewhere. She does not chat as she used to, she merely answers the questions she is asked. S. notices that she has started to repeat certain movements. She sits in the corner, rocking back and forth for long spells, humming a nursery rhyme. Or she keeps rubbing her hands and shoulders nervously, as if she is cold. Or combing her hair. She runs the comb through her hair rhythmically until one of the girls can no longer stand it and gently takes the comb out of her hand. She jumps, suddenly, as if startled out of a dream.

She has long, dark, shining hair. She reminds S. of Snow White. She remembers that in the story Snow White has hair 'as black as ebony'. She does not know what ebony looks like exactly, but seeing A.'s hair, S. imagines that Snow White's must have been just the same. A. washes her hair every day, as if to rinse out her nocturnal fears.

Her mother was killed by soldiers in front of their house. A. heard the soldier shoot. Her mother fell down with her eyes open and fixed on A. Although she did not blink, her eyes were alive for a long time. And it was only because she did not blink that A. knew it was time to go. She turned around and ran. The soldiers shot at her but missed. She was swift and the woods were near. Quite a few people from the village were already in the woods. But after a few days hiding out they were found and taken to a camp. They were discovered because at night they would come back to the village for food. There is nothing edible in the woods, explains A.

She does not know what happened to her brother and father. They were told that all the men had to report to the town hall. One morning they left and she has not seen them since.

She worries most about the dog that was left tied up in the yard. What do you think, what happened to him? she asks. S. says that the dog was bound to have pulled free of his chain and will be freely roaming around the woods hunting rabbits. The thought pleases A. and for a long time she is calm. With T.'s disappearance, A. has no rest, not even when she sleeps. She tosses and turns, raves and sobs. But when someone hugs her she stops immediately. She merely needs to be embraced and she falls sound asleep, like an overwrought child. Sometimes, when she is asleep, she makes a sound reminiscent of small forest animals when they are caught in a trap. The sound wakes S. up at night and then she cannot fall back to sleep.

The soldier who enters the 'women's room' that night knows A.'s name. She is sitting on the mattress, reading a romantic novel which each of them have already read several times. She hears her name and starts in surprise. It has never happened before that an unknown soldier has called any of them by name. A. knows that. S. notices that A.'s hands are trembling as she puts the book down beside the mattress. She casts a quick, questioning look around the room, but all the other girls are just as surprised. Then A. gets up on uncertain feet, as if she might fall. She is wearing a short summer dress. She stands up straight and tugs the hem down. The action reveals her utter confusion and fear.

Two more soldiers are standing in the corridor. They do not enter the room. These soldiers are dressed differently from those who usually come here. Their uniforms are well-cut and new. Black uniforms that she has never seen before.

They have some sort of yellow insignia on their shoulder, like the head of a tiger. Tiger, that's stupid, thinks S. to herself, there are no tigers in Bosnia . . .

Now A. is at the door. The soldier who called out her name offers his hand. He says something to her. She seems to recognise him, as if they know each other. A. turns to the girls. This is a friend of my brother, my brother is alive, she says happily. She looks radiant. The soldier smiles as well. S. remembers how she thought at the time that his smile seemed unpleasantly contrived. Why had he come for her? Where was he taking her? How did he know she was here? S. senses that there is something false about this picture of joy, but she cannot warn A. to be careful.

A. blows the girls a kiss. She blows it into the room as if it were a bubble. For a second, just one more second, she stands at the open door, and then disappears like a ghost. The door closes. The room is still. That's a friend of her brother, one of the girls says, as if trying to reassure them all with her words.

The person who returns to the 'women's room' the following evening is no longer A. None of them recognise her. She looks like her but they immediately realise that this is no longer A., that A. has left the body standing in front of them. Like her mother whose eyes lived on long after she was dead, A.'s body is still alive, but A. is dead. Since the guards brought her back she neither cries nor speaks. She must have been struck dumb because she doesn't make a sound any more. Her eyes are fixed. They blink, but do not see. Her eyes are black holes letting in no light.

A cross and four Cyrillic 's's, like four horseshoes, have been carved with a knife on her chest, forehead and back. There are black clots of blood in the gashes and from afar they look like symbols neatly inscribed in paint. Except that the wound on her back is deep and every time A. moves its pink flesh yawns open. She lies on her side. N. brings over a basin of warm water and the girls wash her clean, weeping. The water in the basin is pale pink, like her cheeks.

A. dies three days later. The wound on her forehead had already started to heal and a fresh reddish scar was beginning to appear under the scab.

The worst thing for me was that this young man really did know her, he had been a friend of her brother.

The 'women's room', Bosnia

JULY 1992

Sometimes, apart from their clothes, the girls also leave behind their make-up. S. finds a plastic cosmetics bag with a clip. Inside it are a bright red lipstick, the sort she herself has never used, a black eye-liner, mascara, face powder, three shades of eye-shadow, and a half-empty jar of Nivea cream. S. is sorry that there is no deodorant inside, none of these village girls use deodorant. She thinks of the girl who collected her belongings from the bathroom without thinking, as if packing for an ordinary trip, the way she herself had done. How could they have known? Yet perhaps they should have known. The rapid movements of a woman's hand, almost automatic. Not knowing. Not understanding. A girl who hopes that she will need lipstick.

Inside are also a comb and a toothbrush. She takes out the toothbrush and looks at it. When someone leaves behind a toothbrush it is a sure sign that that someone will not need it any more.

She is drawn to the cosmetics bag. In Sarajevo she used to put on make-up every morning. When she transferred to the village, she stopped wearing it within a matter of days.

S. takes the lipstick and puts it on. In the small square mirror in the bag she sees the blood-red lips, shiny, white teeth and the tip of her tongue. She smiles and the lips in the mirror smile back. It amuses her that her lips are glossed again. She takes the black eye-liner and carefully draws a line along one eyelid and then the other. She adds the grey eye-shadow and black mascara. Now, looking out at her from the little mirror are mysterious, seductive eyes. She does not quite recognise herself, but that does not bother her. She sees her former face surface, a face she had completely forgotten. As if she is turning herself into another woman by means of make-up, it reminds her that she once lived in a city and she likes that. She feels like the old S. now, getting ready to go out for the evening. She puts on a mask for the present S. to hide behind. She finally realises what it means to be an actress. How wonderful it is to be able to change your face, turn yourself into someone else, if only for a moment. And how simple it is. A touch of red lipstick and already you are a different woman.

Suddenly, she feels liberated. What a relief, to have such a wonderful opportunity at hand. She wants to share it with the other girls. She shows them her made-up face. She cries: look how pretty I am! She twirls around, arms spread out, until she feels dizzy. Breathless, joyful, she throws herself on to the mattress. The discovery that she can conceal herself like this and assume a role suddenly restores her lost self-confidence.

The girls do not understand, they are worried. J. touches her on the forehead. Take off the make-up, she says. You look like a whore. She is standing over her, leaning down as if about to slap her face. M. is angry, she can sense it from the sharp edge to her voice. But why are you angry? S. asks, I *am* a whore. We are all whores. M. wipes the make-up off S.'s face with a wet towel. A red smear is left on the towel.

You don't understand a thing, S. cries out, you are all

dumb peasants! Tears stream down her face. J. steps back, looking at her with horror-filled eyes. She's gone crazy, crazy, she says softly. S. runs into the toilet. She leans against the door. She takes out the lipstick again. They do not understand a thing. She has to explain to them somehow that it is important for them to be able to disguise themselves, that it is a good thing. Her hands are trembling, the red lipstick slides over her lip line.

N. is banging on the door. She understands, S. can tell from her look. You just want to look pretty for our boys, right dear? S. nods her head. N. strokes her hand. Look pretty for the boys, she repeats N.'s words loudly. Of course, so they like you. So you can smile with painted red lips at those boys, those enemy soldiers. Smile and say to them: come into my arms. Quietly swallow the horror, like sperm. Pretend it is not being forced on you but rather that it is fun and you enjoy it. Then perhaps they will forget that their task is to rape you.

Later S. tells the girls that it had not been a moment of madness. She had simply had enough of being nothing more than a piece of stored meat, like a leg of mutton or giblets. Enough of lying around. Of waiting. Of listening out for footsteps, quickly trying to guess how many of them there are. Of nurturing her own fear which, at the sound of familiar noises, flutters in her breast like a crazed bird. A body whose every nerve is strained, already prepared for torture . . . there, that was what she wanted to change. At that moment she had wanted to do something that would make her feel human again. Nothing heroic, nothing that would endanger their lives. Just something within the scope of opportunities offered by the 'women's room'. When she realised that the make-up enabled her to don a mask, she discovered that it was a way to gain power. Yes, she would look pretty for the boys, play with them and thus perhaps deprive them of the chance to humiliate her.

She tries once more to explain to the girls in the room the importance of acting. She tells them that if they pretend they are enjoying themselves, if the soldiers think they are being seduced, then they are powerless to humiliate them. They are no longer men with guns, they are merely ordinary men. The girls do not have to fear that they will catch on to their little game.

S. says all this very seriously and with cool composure. She is not certain that they understand her. She could put it to them more simply, that this might make it easier for them to survive.

When they get to bed, they leave the door to the toilet open. Fresh air comes in through the little window, drops to the floor, caresses S.'s feet and stomach, tickles her neck and climbs up to her nostrils. She inhales deeply, breathing in this bit of fresh air. She hears the song of the crickets and imagines that she is swimming in the sea. It is warm, there is not a cloud in the sky. A pebble beach, pine forest and crickets are off in the distance. And she feels then that she is not in the 'women's room' but somewhere far, far away. An unreal peace pervades the camp at night sometimes.

That night S. is awoken by the sound of coughing. She opens her eyes. It must be early morning, just before dawn. The room is full of smoke, but she can make out M. lying beside her. She is coughing too. It is as if someone has tossed a smelly smoke bomb into the room. It is not the smoke that bothers her so much as the terrible stench. It is an unfamiliar smell which enters the nose, hair, pores. She does not know how to describe it exactly, but it reminds her of scorched meat. Can it be that somebody is burning meat? A dead animal probably . . .

She is tired and wants to go back to sleep but she is choking. S. climbs on to the toilet bowl to close the little window. But M. is already banging on the door to the corridor, calling for someone to unlock the door because they are all going to suffocate. The smoke is not that thick but the smell is making her sick. Someone looks out the bathroom window, shouting fire, fire. Again, S. climbs on to the toilet bowl but all she can see through the window is thick black smoke streaming out of one of the wheelies. Then she sees the fire and dying flames. All the girls are awake now. Air, if only they can get some fresh air. But there will be no draught of air until someone opens the door.

At last, N. unlocks the door. She is still in her blue flowery night gown. The gust of air clears the smoke from the room, but not the smell. N. holds a hanky up to her nose. Her eyes are tearing. What's the matter, what are you making such a fuss for, it's just the garbage they are burning, she says. N. is not alone. She has H. with her. Her eyes are glazed. N. looks as if she came not because the girls made a ruckus, but because H. was unable to come back to the room on her own. She locks them in again. They are alone with the unbearable smell.

H. stares unblinkingly at a fixed point, as if hypnotised. She is as pale as the wall she is leaning against. She looks as if she sees something the others do not. Two soldiers had come for her the night before and taken her away. She had been in a good mood. S. recognises the symptoms of shock and knows that it has to do with the soldiers. H. cannot speak, she just keeps repeating: no, no. Then she sobs, her head bowed.

Daybreak finds them still awake. There is a strange unease

in the room. The girls sense that something unusual is happening. S. feels that they are all in the grip of fear which, like a rash, surfaces suddenly. As the unfamiliar stench continues to choke them, all the terrible, menacing things that surround them daily—the camp, death—suddenly become tangible and visible.

In their small female community, the only reality is what happens to them, to each of them individually. All else becomes incomprehensible. They are completely isolated from the camp's daily life. Here they operate in a special way, as a service, a factory for further humiliating the inmates. Still, they think that they may survive this way. They have learned. They have had to. They know that the other women inmates pity them. They themselves do not have the strength for self-pity; in their situation that is a luxury. Moreover, it seems to S. that with time the girls have become stronger, tougher. Every morning they nurse their fresh wounds, glad to have survived yet another night. Day has dawned, each one of them opens her eyes. Perhaps today they will have a quiet night or fresh bread. Or perhaps there will be shooting in the area, then the soldiers will go out 'into the field' and leave them alone for a while. For the women, happiness is the interlude between horrors.

The smell does not evaporate. They are crowded together like animals, bewildered. S. says that the smell reminds her of burned skin, when she pressed her leg against the stove as a child. She says this in a whisper but H. suddenly jumps with a start. She raises her head. That, that's it, she stutters like an inarticulate child. She begins to shake. They wrap a sheet around her, give her water to drink. She gulps it down as if she cannot believe she is still alive. The water spills down her chin and on to her top. Calm down, you're with us, S. tells her, stroking her damp hair. Finally H.

begins to breathe more evenly. It's true, she says, it's true about the smell. It's the smell of human flesh. The soldiers are burning the corpses of the detainees.

Now she is speaking quite clearly. Her words are met with silence, as if she had never even uttered them or had spoken them too softly. But all the girls are, of course, listening to her. S. watches the expressions on their faces change. First there is disbelief, then horror. It takes them time to realise that this stench, this unbearable smell comes from the burning of human bodies. Can human flesh smell so . . . inhuman?

H. says the soldiers were roaring drunk when they came for her and that, after beating and raping her, they had taken her to the back of the building.

There was a pile of human corpses in the yard, perhaps a dozen or more. The soldiers had made H. look at them. They are your villagers, they told her, that's what we do to them. A bullet in the head and then into the wheelie. Take a look, that's how you'll all wind up, said the youngest and drunkest of the men. H. knows him only too well, they used to work together. Women and children alike, they would all wind up in there if it were up to me, he said.

The guards came and silently tossed the corpses into the wheelie. One of them took a plastic jerrycan of gas and poured it over them. Then he lit a cigarette and tossed in the match. The blue flame shot up into the sky. The soldiers laughed. Look at them burn, they shouted. H. could not bear it any more. She ran for the building. Amused by the sight, the soldiers let her go.

N. watched it all leaning out of her ground floor window. She did not say a word, she simply helped H. up to the room.

S. finds it hard to believe the story at first. How could anyone think of burning corpses in a wheelie for garbage?

She does not accept the idea that death is not the worst thing that can happen to a person, that one can still be humiliated even when already dead. S. feels herself desperately fending off this notion. Their action is terrible not only for the people burning in the pile of garbage, but also for those who lit the match.

They have become accustomed to death. Death is something close to them, something human, even when it is brutal and violent. But burning human corpses in wheelies is something else. It is an unacceptable act. People burning like garbage—and smelling a hundred times worse. Is that the ultimate? Or is there something worse? Feeding the corpses of killed inmates to animals? Perhaps they are already doing that. At this moment of daybreak, as the smell of burning flesh which now has a name fills the room, nothing seems impossible any more. The only thing she understands is that while she may not have much of an imagination, others have too much of one. The fact that she is short on imagination comes as a consolation right now.

And N. told us that it was garbage burning, says J. darkly. Chilling, concentrated hatred pours from her words. It rushes out like a torrent, swirling around the room. At that moment, every girl in the room wants to hate somebody. Only hatred can lighten the burden of what they know.

So, for them, the prisoners are garbage. N. is right, they set fire to garbage. That is what they think. The men killed are not human beings but human garbage, that is why they were killed. S. realises that they are being choked by helpless fury, by the grief that is distorting their faces. Squeezed in the corner, S. feels pressured by the stench and by their now tangible hatred. S. is absolutely certain that at this moment they themselves would be capable of doing the same thing to the soldiers in the yard. Of killing them, setting fire to them, taking pleasure in the flames. She is not even sure about herself, not at this moment. Perhaps she would join them. Perhaps she would be the first to light the match.

S. tries to resist the rush of hatred, she tries to think. She does not want to be like the people who set fire to the corpses in the yard. She tries to say something to the girls, to alleviate the situation. So she says that N. is not to blame. H. gets up and pushes her, shouting. Yes she is, she is to blame, and how! They are all to blame! She watched, I saw her, silently she watched them burn. She did not say a word. She did not close the window. She is to blame, S. concedes, though it is true that they are all to blame, albeit not equally.

What could N. have done? In a way, she is herself a prisoner in this camp. Perhaps she was drunk. S. does not know why she needs to defend N., perhaps she does not even believe what she is saying at that moment, she simply wants to oppose the darkness they are all plunging into.

Well, I've had enough of your understanding for everybody and everything, Teach, H. shouts. I'd stand everybody up in front of a wall and rat-tat-tat-tat, without mercy. Both those who behave like that, and those who defend them. Are you one of us or one of them? Corpses are burning in the garbage bin and you're telling me that she's not to blame? Am I to blame? Did I kill and burn them, little lady?

What could S. say to that? Perhaps that the only difference is that none of them had had the chance to do the same thing. Only then would the women know whether they were any different from the soldiers. But what gives S. the right to judge, when it all boils down to the difference between having and not having done it.

In the suffocating smoke, S. gives up trying to persuade and teach others to distinguish between nuances. She has no desire to defend anybody, she is a prisoner as much as they are. She would like to tell them that, as she sees it, someone who kills a person, someone who lights the match and someone who watches it cannot all be equally guilty. There have to be degrees of guilt, otherwise they are all lost. S. is at least willing to see that N. is powerless, maybe even horrified. What can the old woman do when drunken soldiers are killing prisoners in front of her eyes and setting fire to their corpses? She is the wife of the former watchman of a warehouse for agricultural machines. Perhaps she could have left, one can probably always leave. She must have had the possibility of choice, because every human being has a choice. But what do I or anybody else know about someone else's possibility of choice, thinks S. She can only attest to the fact that in choosing between being kind or being cruel to the women in the room, N. has chosen to be kind, to take real care of them, to bring them bread and soap, to console them. Therein lies her choice. Perhaps she is not strong enough for anything else, for something better or more conscientious. Like so many others, N. perhaps knows that she would have to pay for such a choice with her life. She too is part of the system, part of the camp, rather like the prisoners, a person without a will of her own and without the freedom to decide about her own life. The difference is that, for the time being, no one is going to fire a bullet into her head.

S. also feels the desire for revenge when she thinks about her parents and sister and the man who moved into their apartment. Could she too kill? What would make her behaviour any different? Would her feeling of hatred not simply be the mirror reflection of their own? But this all sounds like self-justification. *Once you suspect that you yourself are capable of doing the same thing, it is already too late. Because you have already imperceptibly taken the first step towards the other side, their side.*

In the morning the room is brighter, the smoke has gone but the smell clings to the body, the walls, their clothes, like a thin film of grime that is impossible to wash off. Even when it does finally disappear, none of them will ever forget it. Just as D. can no longer eat pork. S. remembers the cook said that she had seen pigs in her village snuffling around the corpses of villagers. I haven't been able to eat pork ever since, D. told her. And if I happen to cook pork, every time I ask myself the same thing: did this pig eat human flesh? Pigs make me sick, as if they were to blame, not the people behind it.

It is no use talking, each of the women is alone with herself, with this molten hatred that fires the brain and from which there is no escape. Each of them is without retreat, defenceless against the evil they feel inside.

S. withdraws deeper and deeper inside herself. There must be some boundary line beyond which nothing can touch her, no feeling can reach her, not even the fear of death. She must find some inner chamber within herself where she can lose all awareness of self, of where she is and what she is. Something like death which is not death, but merely a temporary absence from her own self. So that she is not present, not there. Sometimes it works. But it is early morning and all she feels is exhausted. There is very little room left inside her for reason. And even that will soon be gone.

Later, someone says the wheelie is gone. Gone! One by one they climb on to the toilet to check. The courtyard now stands glaringly empty. As if there had never even been a wheelie there. A strange feeling comes over S.; for a moment she is almost prepared to question whether the happenings at dawn had merely been a nightmare or perhaps a group hallucination. But the long tyre-marks of the truck that took the wheelie away is some sort of proof. The other is the stench that pervades the room for days after the event.

The 'women's room', Bosnia

AUGUST 1992

The Captain has nice hands. They are spread out on the table and S. has a good look at them. The nails are neatly clipped. That could be a sign of vanity. Or of neatness, even pedantry. His office shows that he does not tolerate disorder. White walls. Clean floor. Clear desk, except for a sheet of paper and a pencil. From time to time he plays with the yellow pencil. Not impatiently, but rather absentmindedly, as if not sure what to say. He invites her to sit down. Actually he says: please, make yourself comfortable, indicating the chair. She is surprised that a man in the camp should address her using the formal *Vi*. To her, an inmate. Then there are the neat hands, the crisply ironed olive green shirt. The smell of the after-shave which S. greedily inhales.

The Captain obviously sets great store by hygiene and manners. He must believe that in the given circumstances he is doing his utmost to maintain order, work and discipline. The given circumstances are war. The Captain shaves regularly. He addresses the inmates, and perhaps all his subordinates, using the formal *Vi* for 'you'. He believes this is the way to keep war at a decent distance. S. takes all this in as she sits across from him. He is not discussed much in the camp. He lives alone in a wing of the administration building. His wife and child are far away somewhere; he is not from here.

Tell me something about yourself, says the Captain, crossing his arms over his chest. He has dark eyes and short greying hair. If they had met somewhere else and if he were not the camp commander, S. would have admitted to herself that he is good-looking. Sharp features, elongated nose, clearly defined lips, thick eyebrows, clipped moustache.

His request disconcerts her. Talk about myself? Which self?, she asks. She sees that now it is he who is disconcerted. The one from before. Of course. Why would he be interested in how she lives here? He knows all that anyway. You are an educated woman, he says, trying to help her remember that other person. Oh, that! Teacher Training College, she says, and suddenly it all looks so incredible to her. As if that really had been somebody else. The lectures, the fear of exams, the nights spent learning names and dates by heart, how could she have forgotten it all? Clearly, the Captain respects education. A teacher, then? An elementary school teacher, an ordinary elementary school teacher, says S., feeling her face stretch into a stupid smile. He softens too, maybe he understands the absurdity of it. So, Teacher, how did you wind up here?

S. asks him not to call her that. It is utterly inappropriate to her situation, she says. He nods. Regrettably, says the Captain, as if referring to an unfortunate set of circumstances in which he plays not the slightest part. S. tells him how she wound up in a village school where she was standing in for an acquaintance who was on maternity leave. When the soldiers arrived in the village she realised it was too late, they were not interested in her explanations. To be honest, she did not even try to explain anything to them. What could she have said? That she was not from that village? That she came from a mixed family? S. gives a dismissive wave of her hand. No, it was already too late. A mistake, then?, he asks. S.

shrugs her shoulders. The Captain knows that there was no question of a mistake. Like the villagers, she was of the wrong ethnicity. Anyway, no one even checked their names. Which means they knew, even before coming to her apartment, they knew who she was. A mistake? Had she stayed in Sarajevo she might have been killed by a sniper's bullet, like her friend who was crossing the street. She had been carrying water. A passer-by later took the loaf of bread. The water spilled all over the sidewalk, mixing with her blood.

As they talk, the Captain looks at her straight in the eyes. He nods his head again. Perhaps he really does understand. Who knows how he wound up here, whether that was not a fluke as well, thinks S. She is unnerved because she feels a kind of closeness to this man. It must be his aftershave, clean nails and ironed shirt. Because, like her, he is urban-bred.

Light floods the table and the blank sheet of paper provided for taking notes. Again the Captain plays absentmindedly with the yellow pencil and it is obvious to S. that he has no intention of writing anything down, that this is not an interrogation. The paper is dazzlingly blank. S. is quite calm, her fear has vanished. After a brief pause she asks him if he is married, if he is lonely. Are you lonely? She speaks in the coquettish voice of a woman who would gladly invite him to dinner. She does so because she realises that he does not know what to ask her, that she has been called in not for questioning but for company. S. senses it instinctively. The Captain is polite, buttoned-up and, for some reason, unassuming, yet he is the camp commander.

How had she caught his eye? Someone must have drawn his attention to her. Or else he had asked around. The only educated woman in the entire camp. Dressed in a blouse and trousers, her hair washed, she sits unafraid in front of him.

She has make-up on. S. never leaves the room without putting make-up on. She looks like a student. S. reads from his eyes that he wants this woman with her smooth skin and intelligent look, not some peasant woman who whimpers with fear and is lost when approached by even her own husband.

S. knows that she must not waste this opportunity of pleasing the Captain. That would be stupid. What is more, he could have taken her by force, but he did not, S. gives him that much.

The Captain smiles. He has nice, straight teeth. Perhaps he is so un-coercive because he is aware of the effect he has on women, thinks S. Now that she has shed her fear, she likes him more and more. He tells S. that he is married but that his wife and son are back in Serbia. He does not speak of loneliness nor does he ever utter the word, but S. sees that this is what it is. He needs company. Are you free this evening, S. asks him, as if they were in Sarajevo or his home city of Belgrade, and it was merely a matter of choosing a restaurant. He accepts the game and she likes that. He completely relaxes. He takes a cigarette and lights it with an elegant lighter from his drawer. She thinks of asking him how he came by this gold-plated lighter, did he perhaps take it from a prisoner, but she decides to put this thought aside, the same way that he puts the lighter on the table, fully aware of its value.

They are still in his office, but both of them already seem to be forgetting where they are, and are enjoying the fact. As the Captain takes a long drag on his cigarette, S. feels the more superior, as if she is the cat and he the mouse, rather than the other way around. She feels that she has gained the upper hand. Their game of seduction makes the situation easier for her. Men want to be seduced, they want to believe they are being seduced even when they can rape the woman. While pretending to seduce them, and pretending to enjoy it, she forces them to play by her rules. And in so doing she deprives them of their main source of pleasure. The feeling of superiority of a Serb raping a Muslim woman gives way to the feeling of superiority of a man satisfying a seductress. This little female trick turns the Serb into merely a man, and their relationship into an ordinary male-female situation. If only she could explain this to the girls . . . To turn their weakness to their advantage, this is this aim of which S. is becoming so aware as she sits across from the Captain.

Later, when she tells them about her visit to the Captain, the girls get all excited. They discuss it. He is the camp commander, after all. Maybe, through S., they can find things out. J. asks her to inquire about her father who came to the camp with her. She has not had any news of him for some time now. M. thinks that perhaps S. could get the Captain to release her mother. H. says, ask him how long we'll be staying here. S. listens to all their requests, as if truly intending to present them to the Captain as though she has been invited to see him as the representative of the 'women's room', and not to amuse him so that he can forget that he is in some camp in the Bosnian mountains.

They do not seem to understand this. J. offers her her black dress for that evening. S. hesitates, but finally acquiesces. Why not? The dress looks good on her. She gets herself ready carefully for the Captain. And she knows why. She might get something truly useful out of this tryst, although she is still not exactly sure what. She puts on powder, eyeshadow and mascara. She lifts her hair and pins it up. She applies bright red lipstick. This time the girls assist, they do not complain about her make-up. She looks good, says S. about her mask. The girls laugh. They think it is a good joke, to talk about yourself in the third person, as if you were a doll or an actress about to take on a new role. Perhaps they do understand this trick of wearing a disguise after all, when they see that with the help of make-up and clothes you can become someone else.

It strikes S. that not a single girl has asked anything for herself. Why not? Why do they give up on themselves? Is it because of their despair? But they are alive, they are still alive.

The Captain opens the door to his apartment in the administration building. He is wearing a white shirt. Come in, he says simply, as if they have known each other for a long time. This was obviously somebody else's apartment once. Kitchen, living room, bedrooms. S. stops in her tracks. It has been so long since she has seen a normal apartment, an ordinary couch and armchairs, carpet, television set, a laid table. Her eyes well up with tears. She bows her head; she does not want the Captain to see how weak she is.

He pours the wine. S. hopes he does not notice how shaken she is or how her hand is clenching her glass. Cheers, she says. The wine slides down her throat and quickly disperses through her veins. A pleasant warmth comes over her and she begins to laugh too loudly. She knows she is drunk and tells him that she does not need much to get drunk and then she cannot stop laughing. She tells the Captain that she is tipsy already and leans against his shoulder. She touches him. But she has still not had so much to drink as not to know that she must not get completely inebriated; she must not forget her role. If she were to get really drunk she might find herself saying something, it would take just one word to put her at risk. Criminal, for instance. The person who is the commander of this camp cannot be anything but a criminal, even if he personally has never killed anyone, thinks S., drinking down one glass after another. She smiles at him, but already she sees him through a fog.

The wine is strong, or else it seems so to her because she has not had any in so long. She tells herself that she must eat, that food will protect her against inebriation. The Captain serves dinner. S. does not know who made it, N. perhaps, or the cook. Obviously he wants them to be alone and S. is grateful to him for that. She does not want any witnesses to what is happening here.

As they sip their soup, real soup, she takes care not to appear voracious, but to conduct herself the way the Captain would expect of an urban woman rather than a peasant woman or inmate. This dinner is fraught with dangerous traps. S. must take care not to succumb to memories. The potatoes are golden brown, the roast beef smells the way her mother used to roast it. Smells are a dangerous thing, they catapult you back into the past and she is afraid of forgetting where she is. She must focus on the Captain. If she manages to do that, everything will be fine. She closes her eyes and listens to his voice.

The advantage of being with the Captain becomes more and more obvious to her with each passing day. To survive. To sip wine, eat, sleep on clean sheets, to be safe. The Captain may be her chance of survival. She does not even contemplate freedom, that naïve she is not. She simply wants to take advantage of this unexpected opportunity to improve her situation. At this moment, she is not even asking herself whether she is right; good and bad make little sense when it comes to camp life. What is useful to you is good, what is of no use or of direct harm to someone else is bad. S. is certain that her actions are not hurting anyone.

She digs into the food every time. She is starving, but is careful for the Captain not to notice it. One cannot say that they are exactly going hungry in the 'women's room', but the food is always bland and the same—potato soup, beans, pasta, rice, cabbage. The Captain has a good appetite himself, maybe food is the only pleasure he has in this sort of life. What other kind of pleasure can he have? Far away from his family, his friends, his city. Surrounded by death and the barbed wire fence of the camp. What kind of a life is that? He has power, of course, but is that enough? It must be enough if you are a man and if you believe that what you are doing is right. Or if you are obeying orders. She does not ask him these things, she does not dare talk about his 'work'. He warned her against it once and S. has kept to their agreement ever since.

She should hate him. But she does not because with him she manages to believe, if only for a moment, that she is not in the camp. This apartment is a sign that something else exists—civilisation, a world outside the barbed wire of the camp. And no matter how inaccessible that ordinary life may be to her, she wants for a moment to live in its illusion. She thinks the Captain needs the same illusion and that this is why they understand each other. No, S. does not hate him. *On the contrary, to this day she remains grateful to him for those evenings they had.*

That first evening he turns on the television and invites her to sit down beside him on the couch, gesturing with his hand in the same way he would to his wife. Is that what this is about? Does S. remind him of his wife or does he simply want to have a woman by his side? It is an old, black-and-white television. She rests her head on his shoulder in the dark. He puts his arm around her for a while. Curled up together on the couch, they watch an old Hollywood movie in silence. The reality of the camp is swallowed up by the surrounding darkness.

When his hand touches her breast it seems so natural. S. does not resist. The sheets on his double bed smell fresh.

The 'women's room', Bosnia

SEPTEMBER 1992

Yes, the Captain is lonely. He does not talk about it but at least once a week, usually Saturdays, he invites her to keep him company. As if the camp were a business which closes on weekends. He talks to her about his five-year-old son. He shows her a photo of a smiling little boy with a football, and then snapshots from the seaside. The sea, says the Captain pensively, as if doubting that not so long ago he was lying next to his son on the beach. He too doubts his previous life, thinks S. Then he talks about his friends and his sister. He does not mention his wife. Simply because he is being considerate to me, thinks S.

But there is no Saturday or Sunday in the camp, every day is the same. Only he and S. have weekends. Once, on a Saturday evening, a soldier knocked on the apartment door, interrupting their dinner. She heard the Captain swear for the first time. He was gone for approximately an hour. S. watched television in his absence. He said nothing when he returned. He was brooding and angry for the rest of the evening.

The following day she heard that a woman had tried to escape. She was already outside the camp and had almost made it to the woods. The Captain fired the shot himself, furious that a stupid woman inmate had spoiled his quiet Saturday evening.

S. tells herself that she has no other choice than to keep attending these trysts. Which, after the story of the shooting, she finds harder and harder to do. She realises that she can no longer refuse the Captain's invitations. She has consented to this relationship because it makes life in the camp easier; she is exempted from nocturnal visits, and she can sleep and eat better. That is all. She is consciously buying her comfort, bargaining for every minute of time that she spends that way. She admits to herself that she is a coward, but that does not make her feel any better.

The Captain is never rough with her. Still, she is not sure that attraction is the right word for what she really feels, the longing for a normal life, for cosiness. S. sees in him the reflection of that other possible life that someone else must surely be living and that she wants to live temporarily. When she manages to forget where she is. That is something she succeeds in doing, and with each passing day she shrouds herself more and more in oblivion. For S. oblivion is the key to survival.

The only thing I learned in the camp was the importance of forgetting.

And he likes her in the same way. S. senses that he finds in her something different, a small opportunity for possible escape from the camp. Eating together and watching television, talking about childhood, school, movies, cities and travels—about that other, previous life. No, not the news, for God's sake! The news would instil confusion in their false world. S. sometimes risks turning the radio on softly in the kitchen or trying to catch a few sentences on the television which might give her some idea about what is happening in the outside world. She does not understand them, and depends more on what she hears from the girls, and they themselves hear from the soldiers or guards. War is still a nightmare, but now that nightmare is her only reality. And if the war were about to end, would the Captain tell her?

Her relationship with the Captain started with his lust. But with the passage of time this lust has increasingly turned into a closeness of two bodies without desire. Except, perhaps, the desire for neither of them to be where they are. S. quickly falls asleep in his arms. She remembers the touch of his warm skin, his clean smell, the pleasure of that moment when she slips into day-dreaming. She is no longer in the camp then, and that is the only important thing. Outside the wind is howling, the rain sometimes lashing at the windows. S. cuddles up to him, stealing his warmth. She wants to make herself as small as possible, to transform herself into a child, virtually to disappear.

Sex in her life implies violence, unbearable roughness, repulsion. She feels forever soiled by the camp sex. She is convinced that her hair smells of sperm and spit. She keeps washing herself with soap and hot water because at his place she has both, and a real bath tub at her disposal, but the smell is still impossible to wash off. Every time she showers in his bathroom she wonders whether the Captain notices the smell of other men on her skin, the trace of their odour that has permeated her body. Does it bother him, or does it excite him? That male sharing in the humiliation of women, that male fraternity of theirs as they watch each other doing it—does that excite them?

Her relationship with the Captain marks an advancement in her camp status. She is now exposed to the whims of one man only. That is a plus for a woman from the 'women's room'. A step forward in self-preservation. As she gets ready to visit him, she almost wants to congratulate herself on her artfulness.

Once, as she is getting ready to go to the Captain, J. says

out of hearing of the others: you've sold yourself cheap. She says it to her face, without any hatred, as a fact which she would have to take into account henceforward. S. wonders whether J. knows something or is simply guessing. S.'s visits to the Captain mean respite to her, but she realises that this makes for a rather weak defence. She feels as if J.'s words have been stamped on her brow. Perhaps not so cheap, she replies in the same voice.

Of course, S. stands out. She is marked by him having chosen her. The girls in the room cannot be indifferent to the fact. S. is still in the room with them, she still sleeps with them. She knows it bothers them that she is no longer the same as them. The fact is that S. is not at the disposal of the soldiers any more and in the 'women's room' that is a privilege. S. thinks that the girls envy and despise her for it. The make-up, acting like a real whore . . . she is the only real prostitute among them, and that is how she feels, too. It is no use explaining to J. that it was a fluke that the Captain picked her rather than someone else. She can ask the tired question yet again: what would you have done in my place? No one, not even the girls in this room, has the right to judge her, thinks S. to herself. Her choice at that moment seems to her perfectly rational.

S. lies to the girls that the Captain is making her go to him, that he is threatening her. They pity her. S. endures the hypocrisy of her position in silence. She knows that she does not deserve their attention and pity, but she dares not admit it to them. She goes to that man voluntarily and behaves towards him as though toward an acquaintance who is doing her a favour by making her stay in the camp that much more bearable. Except she is at all times aware of her guilt, her hypocrisy.

She does not know how to explain to the girls their tacit

agreement, the joint fostering of the illusion of normality which both he and she need. This means no mention of camp life when they talk, not a single word. That is why she cannot inquire about this person or that, she cannot intercede on anyone's behalf. Her hands are tied by their agreement. Does that mean complicity? Is she still a victim, like the others? She is already accustomed to the situation, to the visits, baths, food, his touch, his smell. To his childhood stories and excerpts from his son's letters which he reads aloud to her. The first time she tried to discuss the war with him she could feel him stiffen. I'm a soldier, I've got no choice. The Muslims want a state of their own, like the Croats, he told her. It was a warning not to raise the subject again. The next time they met he asked her not to talk about the war or his job. She understood that as part of their bargain.

S. is convinced she cannot ask the Captain for any protection for the others. She thinks she can only try to protect herself. What would somebody else do in her place? Still, she thinks of E. and her daughter. She does not see them often any more. If S. were ever to ask for help for someone else, it would be for those two.

But she cannot conceal from herself the fact that she is sleeping with a murderer. At daybreak, as the birds awaken, she makes herself sick. Sometimes she thinks she would have enough strength in her hands to finish him off. At that moment, caught between night and day, when his sleeping body is utterly at her mercy, she looks down at her hands. She knows where he keeps his pistol. It is a moment of total consciousness, when she knows what she ought to do; it would be a simple execution of justice, nothing more. Her whole being cries out for atonement by this act. A chill runs down her spine. She feels an impotence and limpness in her arms that is not due to sleepiness. On the contrary, S. is utterly awake, all her senses alert. The limpness comes from her weakness, her incapability. She knows that she will not take advantage of the opportunity, ever. The birds are awake now, in a few seconds the Captain will open his eyes to make sure that she carries out his order. He will not get up, he will not even watch her leave.

She always leaves his bed at the crack of dawn. That is the deal. Around four in the morning, five at the latest, he wakes her up and, like a servant, S. obediently gets up, leaving her smell behind on the crumpled sheet, which he pulls to his side. If she turns around, she will see his sleeping face, his past life and present lie. In the languid movements of his sleeping body, in his even breathing, in the cold air of the room, she will see, if she but turns around, the reflection of death on his face. At that instant of daybreak, S. senses what the sleeping man does not yet know, that he is, after all, a condemned man.

S. steps out of the room, closing the door softly behind her, so as not to wake him. The corridor leading to the 'women's room' is dark. The camp is still asleep. Yet another day is dawning when the Captain, undisturbed, will get on with his work, as he refers to running the camp.

Of course, at the heart of it was the fear that I would have to pay for such an act with my own life, the fear that killing him would at the same time mean my own suicide.

Inmates do have a choice, except that it may sometimes mean death. One woman tells her what she saw when she was helping out in the kitchen at the men's camp one day. The kitchen overlooks a patch of land which was once a football field. The guards sometimes take the prisoners out there to have their fun with them. That day they brought out a small group of men. Some of them were very young, boys really. One of the guards beckoned to an older man, shortish and frail-looking. He stepped out of the group, his head bowed. Then the guard called over a boy. He ordered them to strip naked. The boy had to get down on his hands and knees and stay like that on all fours. His pale, thin body shook at the laughter of the guard, as if he were being beaten. One of the guards took a pistol and pressed it against the older man's head. The man got down on his knees behind the boy, and then fell on to his side, whimpering like a wounded dog. The guard shot the boy first and then the man.

Immediately afterwards, when they called out the next boy and man and ordered them to do the same thing, the man dropped to his knees without giving it a second thought. The guards gave him brandy to drink. He had to rape the boy repeatedly, until he ran out of strength and the boy fainted.

Later she heard that the two men who had been killed, like the two who had survived, were father and son.

I watched all that and then I thought of my husband of whom I have no news and of my son who died of his wounds in my arms, and I wished they would kill me too, says the woman.

After a while, the daily horrors and death become routine. S. listens to the camp stories without emotion, she listens to the words dropping into the hollow of her insides. Or she sees scenes, sees them with her own eyes, but it is as if they do not directly concern her. She is no longer horrified or saddened, she does not react at all. Death surrounds her daily, death is a fact. But it is also something that does not concern her until the moment it touches her personally. S. is convinced that the only way to survive in the camp is this, to look the other way. Help if you can and if there is a point, the way the girls helped her when she was brought badly battered back to the room. Yet she knows that she cannot prevent anyone's death, anyone's rape, and this knowledge saps her of the strength to even try. A particularly cruel story will snap her out of it for a second, but then she slumps back down under the weight of impotence and daily life in which it is each woman for herself. She is sometimes amazed by her own capacity for self-oblivion, resistance, resilience and her desire to survive. She feels that for her as well, life has imperceptibly and against her will become a force beyond her.

But even we victims acted as though it could not be otherwise, thus closing the circle with the criminals. As if we existed only within that room and camp. As if for us the outside world had completely disappeared and there was only one single rule in camp life: to survive, to survive whatever the cost.

The 'women's room', Bosnia

OCTOBER 1992

It is autumn already. At night the cold nips at your fingers. The grass has turned yellow and in the early morning a thick fog blankets the surrounding meadows. A little wood-burning iron stove is in their room now and N. lights it every so often, usually in the evening. There is no mention of leaving or of being exchanged any more. S. remembers when she came, when she still believed that they could not be staying here for long. Why couldn't they? And what does *long* mean now, when their notion of time and space has so utterly changed?

The first rumour of an exchange comes one morning. N. says she heard it from her husband, and swears it is the truth. The girls do not dare believe her. She smiles kindly, that does not surprise her. No wonder they do not know what to think, it would be dangerous to believe news like that. It might raise their hopes. S. is afraid of futile hope spreading through the camp like a fever. Still, she notices that at the slightest hint of such a possibility, a current of happiness runs through her entire body like a wave of heat. Exchange! To leave here, this room, this camp . . .

They have to be patient and wait for the news to be confirmed by some other source. Several days later, the same news arrives from the kitchen. Now it is almost official, there is going to be an exchange. But they cannot tell from the news exactly what awaits them, whether all the women will be exchanged or just those in the 'women's room'. After such a long time the news seems unreal to them. They are now eight in the room and not one of them knows exactly what to do with this news. Should they hope? S. certainly wants to leave the camp, they all do. But where will they send them? To some other camp, and then—where? At the thought of the uncertainty of this new situation, happiness surprisingly quickly gives way to apprehension. And S.'s first reaction is fear, as if she already finds it difficult to imagine something else, a different life from that of the camp.

She feels like a sick animal which has dug itself a little hole in the ground to hide in . . .

Although it is still not yet official, news of the exchange spreads, arousing suppressed memories and disturbing their daily routine. M. talks about her husband whom until now she believed dead. Even though she has had no news of him, she now thinks he might be alive after all. S. thinks of her parents. As if frozen until now, she feels the ice inside her slowly start to melt. She has had no news of her family either; she believed that their disappearance meant that they were dead. But now she feels she can allow herself to hope. For the first time in a long time the girls dare to contemplate the future.

The anticipation changes the atmosphere in the room. The girls become increasingly edgy. They argue over every little thing, over whose turn it is to do the washing, over the soap, over the bread. They ask S. to check the news with the Captain, who must know whether it is true or not. Rumours spread through the camp like wildfire. From the kitchen to the warehouse, the 'women's room', and the administration building. It is no longer an exchange, it is the army, 'our' army, which is approaching and which will liberate all the prisoners. They hear that the killings in the other camp have been stepped up. Short bursts of gunfire can be heard at night, a sure sign of elimination. Sometimes in the early morning hours, S. sees through the toilet window guards in the distance loading corpses on to a truck. The corpses are as rigid as logs. The fact that for the time being they are liquidating only the men from the other camp is no consolation to her. Instead of the order for the women to be exchanged, the camp could receive a different kind of order . . .

S. is cautious with the Captain. She does not ask him directly, but tries to show that she is visibly upset. The Captain cannot but notice that S.'s mind is elsewhere, that she is silent, that she merely responds to questions asked, that she does not laugh as she usually does. This goes on for several evenings. Finally, he broaches the subject. S. tells him that she has heard talk of an exchange. He confirms it. He says he meant to give her the good news, but that he is still not one hundred per cent certain. The Muslims are holding some important people of theirs and are asking for a certain number of civilians in return. The negotiations are still in progress. We will send them only women, says the Captain. Does that mean they are trying to get rid of the male inmates, completely liquidate them? S. asks the question spontaneously, the words simply spill out and it is too late to take them back. This outburst of courage surprises the Captain. He simply stares at her without answering. Perhaps it is already too late for him to react, perhaps he himself has already abstained from the lying in which they both take part.

At the end of October, the Captain finally says that the women will be leaving the next day. S. holds her breath. She wants to shout with excitement. She does not believe it, she dare not believe it, because she will again do something imprudent and spoil everything. She must not say a word. She remains seated although she can feel her knees shaking. She asks him for a glass of brandy. She knocks it back, like a pill.

It occurs to her just then that the women being exchanged need not be those from the 'women's room'. Indeed, it would be logical to get rid of such awkward witnesses. Why had she hoped at all? Now the sudden surge of hope is suffocating her, like a dull pain spreading from her chest all over her body. She feels hot. She is sick. She is absolutely sure she is sick. She has not an ounce of energy left, all of it has vanished at this dreadful thought.

S. is overcome by the thought, it gives her no peace. Even alcohol does not help. The remains of dinner are on the table. Chicken bones, cabbage salad, slices of bread, rice. Suddenly she sees that her cautious behaviour with the Captain is completely superfluous now. This is the end. The illusion of normality has been shattered. She is gnawed to the bone, like those chicken bones on the plate. The war is laughing in their faces and the Captain sees it. It is pointless now to keep quiet about herself, about them.

The smell of burning lard, which never used to bother her before, wafts in from the kitchen. She notices particles of dirt on the edge of her plate that make her stomach turn. The smell of the vinegar in the salad suddenly invades her nostrils. S. feels she needs air. She becomes short of breath, as if she is choking. She recognises the signs of panic.

And me, what about me, she finally manages to say. Her words roll around the room for a while unanswered, as heavy as lead balls.

S. weeps. The Captain wipes away her tears and then holds her face in his hands for a long time. You will be going too, all of you will be going, don't worry. S. still weeps. She knows that she should not rely completely on his words because he could change his mind or be given different orders or be replaced . . . But at that moment her hopes are so strong that they squeeze out all other emotions. For the first time in a long time the word tomorrow seems to have some meaning. She can hear the erratic fluttering of her own heart and she clearly senses a new fear, fear of that same tomorrow.

As she leaves that evening, the Captain perhaps senses that he is seeing her for the last time. He strokes his chin hesitantly and S. notices that he has not shaved for several days. He says he will look her up one day, yes he will, when this is all over. She has the strength for just one last false smile. Do, by all means, look me up, she says.

They are leaving, they are going to Croatia. Actually they are being transferred to another camp, a refugee camp outside Zagreb. She has a second cousin in Zagreb, maybe the woman could help her out. Although she does not know whether she will be able to stay in Zagreb. They say Croatia is not accepting any more refugees, that it is sending them on to Slovenia, to Germany, to Scandinavia. But S. cannot think now about what will happen if she cannot stay in Croatia, that is all too far off, too unreal.

They are all gripped by tension pending their departure, by the fear that there will be a snag, that at the last minute the two sides will break off the negotiations. And by the uncertainty, but a different kind of uncertainty, one mixed with the happy expectation of what she dares not call freedom.

For the third time, S. takes out her backpack and packs the remainder of her belongings. There are far fewer of them now. She gave the notebook and pencils to E.'s daughter. They stole her little box with what was left of her jewellery. All she has now is some underwear, her photo album, toothbrush, the red dress she never wore and her still pristine Italian shoes.

It is cold and none of them had come prepared for winter. N. had supplied her with a sweater made of peasant wool. She did not say where she got it; perhaps in the next village, perhaps she had knitted it herself or taken it off someone thinking it was a pity for it to go to waste. S. decides to trade her fine shoes for a jacket. D., the cook, takes the shoes. She is so young, so vivacious that spring seems just around the corner to her, within reach. The jacket she gives S. in their swap is too big, obviously a man's jacket. No one needs the red dress and S. returns it to the bottom of her backpack.

Wherever she is going she will need money. Money is obtainable in the camp, you just have to have something valuable to sell, but S. has nothing, not a thing.

They will be leaving at the crack of dawn, that they now know. The soldiers have not appeared for several evenings now, and that is reason enough for them to be in a good mood. Their last evening in the 'women's room' is somewhat unreal, as if they are all here but also already somewhere over 'there', in an unknown world. Separated. S. knows that she may never see any of these faces around her again. Here, in this room, they were together. They knew each other, became used to each other, and that gave them a sense of safety and the strength to go on. That evening the girls are kind to each other, aware that life, which threw them together in this room, is about to part them.

S. feels that she is losing something and that, in her effort to forget the bad, she will forget the good things that tie her to these women.

It is warm. There is the aroma of freshly made coffee that N. obtained somehow, a farewell gift for the girls. They are sitting around the stove, their bags packed. They have already forgotten this place, their little habits, their spats, the soldiers. The pain, something none of them wants to remember, is not so easy to forget. The scars, both visible and not, remain. Imprinted on the inside of their thighs, their bellies, necks, breasts, wombs, on their minds . . .

S. is sitting by the stove. She feels warm, as though she is waking up from a long numbness, and something inside her is finally coming back to life.

She is leaning against the wall. Tablecloths still cover the windows, keeping out the light. And there they will stay, thinks S. They will leave, and the empty room will remain. As will that other room with the iron bed, and the offices, and the cellar with its blood-stained walls. And N. What will happen to her, to her husband, to the Captain? Whom will he command now? Will there be new women prisoners coming? Is the war still on?

As usual, there is only one light bulb burning. M. is adding stitches, as if in a hurry to finish her knitting before the trip. H. is smiling, her eyes closed. J. is smoking, her mind elsewhere. Two girls are lying down, talking softly, they are going to Slovenia, their parents are there. L. and V. are playing cards. Their time together, this room, the events that intertwined their fates, are still a bond. S. looks at them. They already look remote to her, like a slowly fading painting on the wall.

N. wakes her up in the middle of their last night in the camp. S. thinks it is time to leave and reaches for her backpack. But the other girls are still fast asleep. N. is standing over her with a flashlight and signals for her to follow her out quietly. It is a cold night. The moon is shining down ominously on the icy concrete of the courtyard.

S. opens the door of the room on the ground floor of the

administration building. The room looks like an improvised clinic. Standing at one end is a metal bed, next to it a table with some instruments on it and a screen. E. is lying in the bed. She has only a sheet covering her and S. thinks that she must be cold. The greyish neon light falls on her face, on her closed eyes, on the fair long hair spilling over the pillow and on her arms lying alongside her body. Her skin is ashen. S. steps up to the bed and touches her. E.'s hand is icy cold. Poison, says N., pointing to a small bottle on the metal cabinet.

S. stands next to the bed, holding E.'s cold hand. She does not let it go, as if trying to give her warmth. She looks at her face, with its veil of absence that comes only with death, and she does not understand, she simply does not understand what happened to E. since they last saw each other. She understood the other deaths, she could justify them to herself, there was a logic to them. But she cannot comprehend the death of this woman. She feels lost, cheated somehow. How could the very person in whose strength she had believed the most do such a thing?

E. would sometimes appear in the 'women's room' if one of the girls fell ill. She would give them pain-killers or antibiotics if she had any. Or she would dress their wounds and treat their bruises. She was the only person in the camp who knew how and she therefore had access both to the girls and to the administration building. Sometimes she was also called to the nearby men's camp. She and Z. ate in the kitchen and later were given permission to move into the little room off the kitchen, together with D. the cook. She did not talk much. She would carry messages to and from the men's camp, and sometimes she would bring to the 'women's room' news she had heard about the fighting, about the international forces being sent by the United Nations. It was from E. that she had heard about the siege of

Sarajevo, about the hunger, the bread and water queues, the snipers targeting children and the people who had cut down all the trees in the city parks for firewood. First they burned the books, she remembers E. telling her. E. had somehow managed to maintain contact between the camp and life outside.

S. is used to events in the camp being unpredictable, and usually inexplicable as well. She looks down at the bare concrete floor and at the pair of shoes E. had placed neatly together before lying down in bed, at the skirt and jacket she had hung on the back of the chair before swallowing the poison, at the greenish walls of the narrow room. She should not have done it on this last night. She absolutely should not have done it having already endured all this time, four full months of camp life. E. knew about the bus, about the exchange. The other day S. had run into her in the corridor on her way to the Captain and she had greeted her cheerfully. I'm so happy we're leaving, E. had said to her then, as they passed each other.

N. hands her a letter, a folded piece of paper ripped out of the notebook. It is addressed to S. She unfolds the paper and sees that the letter is very brief:

> *Dear S., Forgive me. I am the one who took your gold jewellery, yours and the other women's. I did it for my little girl. I used it to bribe the soldiers to leave her alone. I hope you understand. Yesterday I realised that all my efforts to spare her were in vain. I can't go on. Goodbye, Love, E.*

Enclosed with the letter was a one hundred Deutschmark bill and her daughter's notebook filled with drawings.

S. sits down on the bed. From up close, E. looks as if she

is asleep. Except she is cold, unbearably icy cold. Why didn't she tell me, S. wonders, as if the answer to that question would be of any help to her now in understanding E.'s act. Of course S. would have given her the gold jewellery, if only she had told her, had explained why. Remembering how bitter she was when she discovered the theft, she is now overwhelmed by embarrassment at her own selfishness. How short-sighted she had been! When she had bemoaned the theft, E. had looked down and S., well she remembers, had taken that as a sign of indifference on E.'s part, as a sign that she had reconciled herself to fate. If only E. had given S. some indication, perhaps it would have made it easier for them both. Perhaps they could have helped each other. These thoughts run through S.'s mind as she sits on the bed next to the dead E. At the same time, she knows it is not certain, not at all certain that she would have given E. the gold jewellery, that she would have understood her fear for her daughter. It never occurred to S., not even for a moment, that the child was at risk. Now she blames herself for such blindness, such insensitivity. The child is not even twelve years old, she is tiny, so thin she is almost invisible. She is still a child, S. says first to herself, and then aloud. And for this to happen now, at the end. What an injustice, that is the only word for it, the only one that comes to mind.

It is getting increasingly cold in the room. The coldness is creeping up her legs and if she stays here much longer she too will turn into a corpse. The bluish white of dawn appears at the window. The day of their liberation, the moment they have been waiting for. It is now here, entering the room, flooding it with a light that only makes S. colder. She feels tired, so tired that she would be happiest if she could just lie down next to E., hold her in her arms and sleep the same sleep.

N. is shaking her by the shoulders. She does not realise that N. has been present in the room the entire time. They have to go back, it is almost time to leave. As they walk down the corridor she sees that the women are already assembling in the courtyard. In the early dawn of winter they look like a flock of birds pressed together.

S. thinks that E.'s little daughter is there among them. Who will take care of her now, she wonders. She stops and looks out the window. Is the girl among them, she asks. N. shakes her head, quickly crossing herself several times. That gesture of the head and hands says it all, explains everything. She is dead, says N., they raped her. Last night.

S. does not want to know any more. But she was still just a child, S. keeps saying, as if her words had any meaning.

The two of them will stay here, buried near the camp. And a part of S. will remain buried here with them. She will leave all these painful memories behind under this shroud of mist, in the earth, in this place between the hills and the woods, surrounded by barbed wire. S. knows that just under the thin layer of earth lie human bones and that one day they will surface and lie white in the sun for all to see, even if they forget the evil inflicted upon them.

She has waited so long to leave. But suddenly she is no longer sure she has the strength for a new life.

Bosnia

NOVEMBER 1992

Is this exchange an end to the war? Or is it merely an end to life in the camp? What awaits them now? What does peace look like? S. cannot imagine what peace might mean for all these women who have no place to go back to and yet are jostling to leave for the unknown. There is no news, no news of peace, in any event. Somebody would have already told them. S. is not sure she will know how to recognise it if she ever lives to see it. The word peace is never mentioned.

The women clamber on to the bus in a panic. S. remembers how quiet and submissive they were when they boarded the bus a few months ago. Now the guards are shouting to what seem to be deaf ears. They are living their last moments in the camp in mortal fear that they will be left behind, that someone or something will stop them, prevent them from boarding. The guards cannot be believed, not even now when the buses are already here. There may not be enough seats for them all, so they had better push their way on and grab one. They are in a panic. They trip and fall. The driver shouts and shuts the door. A woman hangs caught in the door. As if there is no end to their struggle. The scene makes S. want to cry, she is on the verge of tears. This is not how she imagined their departure. She starts feeling better only when she sees J. waving happily. Her bright, smiling face brings relief. It looks as if they are going to have a sunny day for their journey.

As the crammed buses set off slowly down the path leading out of the camp, S. thinks she sees the Captain standing at a window of the administration building. She immediately turns her head away. Just a little bit longer and the Captain will cease to exist. He is just part of a disappearing world which, in her new world, no one will even believe existed. For the second time now, her life is somehow losing its credibility.

They have already turned the bend in the road, they can no longer see the camp. She is plagued by the feeling that with each passing minute there is less and less in her life for her to hold on to with any certainty.

Their driver is a young man in a camouflage uniform. His face is red, and he is perspiring from the effort of trying to keep the bus on the winding mountain road. He is not very adept at driving on such roads. He used to drive a taxi in V. before the war. He says the border is not far away, a two- or three-hour drive at most. Croatian buses will be waiting for them there. If everything goes well, he adds cautiously.

S. listens to the driver say the word 'war'. He says it as if it were a perfectly ordinary word, but even after all these months in the camp, S. is still not quite used to it.

It is cold in the bus. The women press together. They do not dare say anything because this is now freedom. You cannot object to freedom.

The mountain road winds its way down and now the road passes through a valley, alongside a wide murky river. The driver says he will leave them at the Sava River crossing, that is the arrangement. Croatian territory is on the other side.

The place finally appears behind a bend in the road. The bridge has been almost completely destroyed. Slabs of concrete protrude on either side of the riverbank. The buses stop at the crossing and the women alight. A raft and guide are waiting for them. S. looks at the rapids; it is a fast river and it frightens her. This is not how she imagined freedom. Truth be told, she did not imagine anything in particular.

Standing on the other side of the river are soldiers wearing the same camouflage uniforms. But the buses that are to take them to the refugee camp somewhere outside Zagreb have yet to arrive. Are they really safe now? A clamour. The uncertainty spreads like wildfire. What will happen now? Perhaps they have been tricked and there won't be any exchange? Perhaps they are still in Bosnian territory? One of the women sits down on the ground and bursts into tears of despair, as if there has just been a death in the family. She can no longer bear the tension, the waiting. S., too, is upset and tired of waiting. The women stand on the riverbank by the demolished bridge. None of them are dressed for winter, though S. is better off than most. They shiver from the cold, their feet sinking into the wet ground. The commander walks over to them and tells them that everything will be all right. They must be patient, they can't turn back now anyway. They will be given something to eat, just a bit more patience. The buses are arriving tomorrow, for sure. Why, you've survived the camp, you'll somehow survive tonight as well, he says, trying to give them courage.

He cannot understand our exhaustion, thinks S. And the fear that they are still not safe, that someone will come and tell them to go back across the bridge, to return to the other side. And that the same buses will be waiting for them there, as if it had all been a cruel joke. Perhaps the commander does not know that they are all terrified, because they themselves do not realise that waiting, the mere possibility of waiting for something, is in itself freedom. Now they dare to hope and that makes it all the harder for them. Their previous despair was nothing more than bare survival. Breathing, that is all, but they had become used to it. Or maybe the commander does know, but what can he say to console them?

S. watches how the girls from the 'women's room' cling together even now, when there is no need for it any more. They are used to each other. Once condemned to each other, they now sit together as friends. Perhaps it will always be that way, they will all be marked by their common experience and will, in a way, remain bound together. She can barely recognise some of them now that they are outside the room. She notices that H. has covered her head with a kerchief, tied the way peasant women do. She is surprised, she has forgotten that H. is actually a peasant woman. J. offers her an apple. Where did she get that from? S. wonders, as if they were still back there, inside. All the same, she is grateful to J. for the friendly gesture.

The soldiers gather twigs and try to light a fire. They are obviously going to have to spend the night here by the river. There is a destroyed, abandoned village nearby, they'll put them up there.

The twigs are wet, the smoke stings their eyes. A young man in a red cap keeps trying to fan the flame, then gives the little smoking pile of wood an angry kick. He gives up. An older woman works on the fire slowly, patiently. Crouching, she keeps blowing at it until the sparks catch a few of the dry twigs. You can see she is used to doing it, perhaps this is how she used to make a fire in the hearth at home every morning.

Soon the tea is ready. Bread and liverwurst from the soldiers' rations is their first meal in freedom. S. eats the dry piece of bread which crumbles in her mouth. That first dinner outside the camp is so tasty, like at school when the bell rings for break and the cook hands her a freshly baked slice of bread. S. thinks of school—her school in Sarajevo. That is what they ate almost every day, bread and liverwurst. The soldier hands her another thickly spread slice of bread and for a moment she lapses into the past. The smell of the wooden benches in the classroom, the chalk on her fingers. She is sitting by the window, it is raining outside. It is warm and safe in the classroom.

A moment of peace is restored. The liverwurst melts on the roof of her mouth. She washes down the food with large gulps of tea. She clenches the tin mug containing the hot, sweet liquid and tries not to think about tomorrow. It is enough that she feels good now, that she is warm, that she is not hungry.

They come for her in the night to help deliver a baby. A girl from the camp has gone into labour in one of the destroyed houses. The women have spread out an army blanket on the ground. Someone has lit a fire in the corner. The soldiers have given them a petrol lamp.

S. walks in and sees in the circle of light the girl stretched out on her back. Her eyes are closed and every so often she sobs softly. Her mother sighs and crosses herself, saying, my poor girl, my poor girl, what am I going to do with you. Then she leaves S. to keep an eye on the girl and, together with another woman, goes out to the back of the house. S. thinks she can hear the dull sound of a shovel against the earth.

The mother returns. For a while, the girl seems to have calmed down. S. holds her hand and wipes the sweat from her forehead. Then there is a protracted scream. First the girl squeezes S.'s hand hard, then suddenly releases it. It is over. Her mother takes the infant into her arms and carries it away. Now comes the baby's cry, thinks S. But they hear nothing, the silence in the room is as if everyone has suddenly fallen asleep. In the corner, the girl's mother removes the black kerchief from her head and wraps it around the tiny, premature little body. But not as she would with a new-born child; rather she wraps up the entire body, along with its helplessly hanging little head. Before wrapping it up completely, she holds it in her hands for a moment. By the light of the petrol lamp, S. sees the tiny little package lying in the huge hands. The woman seems to be in two minds. Perhaps she pities this little life, its sorrowful fate. They bury the new-born child in the hole they dug in the dark. They place stones on top of the shallow grave. The mother comes back and gently strokes her daughter's cheek. Don't be afraid, sweetie, she says, it's over. It's better this way . . .

The woman beside S., who helped deliver the baby, whispers to her that the girl had been raped even before the camp, while still at school. When she came back to her family in the village, she did not say anything, they would not have believed her. Things like that were happening even then, down in the valley. Meanwhile we were tilling the land and sowing as if absolutely nothing was going on, says the woman. The girl did not tell her mother until they were in the camp. S. does some mental arithmetic: if the child was born prematurely, then what the woman says could be true. So the girl's mother decided it had to die. It would not have survived anyway, it was no bigger than a loaf of bread, it was this big. She shows with her hands how tiny the freshly buried body was.

S. cannot go back to sleep all night. She had been calm until now. She had believed that she could not get pregnant because she had lost her period soon after arriving in the camp. The sight of childbirth has upset her. The same could happen to any of one of them, any one of the girls from the 'women's room'. She is pretty sure that none of the other girls have had their period either, perhaps they too had lost it because of the way they lived in the camp, because of the strains to which they were exposed, because of the fear. In their room, as in the entire camp, pregnancy was not something you could hide, could just keep quiet. But they did not talk about it, at least not in front of S. She understood that they thought of her as being different from them. Not merely because of the Captain, but also because she was a city girl. She remembers how E. had told her that peasant women still refer to their period as 'the female ailment', and to sex as 'it'. One night she heard H. vomiting in the toilet. She was going to get up to help but M. pulled her back down on the mattress.

Not one of them was unconcerned about whether they would leave the camp with a swelling stomach. They had to think about such things. They had to feel changes in their own bodies. Or were their bodies already so bruised and battered, so much not their own, that they were barely capable of noticing any change? Perhaps they concealed such things from each other and did not talk about it because they were perfectly aware of their own helplessness. There was no way to terminate a pregnancy, yet they could not imagine having a child conceived in this way. She remembers the stories of the women in the warehouse. To give birth to a child conceived by rape would be more disgraceful than betrayal for them, a fate worse than death.

What if she has lulled herself into a false sense of security? What if her feeling is wrong? A faint bleeding had appeared just once in the 'women's room', but she was sure that was the consequence of having been raped. She suddenly feels a chill run down her back. Hadn't the girls told her that she had gained a bit of weight? But that was because she was eating well with the Captain . . . She'd know, of course, she would feel it if she were pregnant. S. tosses and turns on the floor and then sits up, gazing into the dark.

She remembers that one evening, before she had fully realised that this was not a subject of conversation, she had asked M. what she would do if she got pregnant. M. had put down her knitting, bowed her head and, for a moment, said nothing. If that were to happen to me I would simply strangle the child with my own hands, M. replied. Her tone implied that this was her final verdict, one that brooked no argument. S. remembers how at the time she had made a gesture with her hands, as if wringing the neck of a little animal, a chicken or bunny. S. will never be able to erase that picture from her mind, the picture of those hands forming a fist and then that short, ruthless snap.

We're not human any more, thinks S., the camp has stopped us from feeling human. How will we ever get used to living outside the camp again? So much unhappiness all around her, she no longer feels capable of goodness or of experiencing beauty. Perhaps what she feels, lying there curled up under the dirty blanket, inhaling the dust, in a house once inhabited by people, on a journey into the uncertain, perhaps it is not simply sadness, but hatred as well. Lying at the bottom of the sadness, like bitter dregs.

She feels trapped. A mechanism is closing in on her which turns humans into non-humans and she is beginning to operate exactly as she is expected to. She sees with horror that, like everyone else, she too is prepared to hate. Opening up inside her again is the hole that swallows up everything that is human about her.

She attended the murder of a child who had done nothing wrong; it had met its death before even taking a breath.

Not a breath in this world. As if they had not seen enough death, the women acquiesce to the same logic of violence which says that *ours* means life and *theirs* means death. They themselves are becoming capable of killing and that is the victory of the logic of war. What hurts S. even more than the quiet death of that tiny being who no one will ever know existed, is the cruelty of the girl's mother. Why did she say that it is better this way?

S. tosses and turns on the dusty concrete floor. The ruins offer scant protection against the winter. Once, perhaps not so long ago, this was a real house. Buried under the bricks in the corner are the remains of plates, empty cans, beer bottles, garbage. It is now an abandoned roofless house. Walls with gaps where the sockets were yanked out, a hole where the toilet bowl once stood, gaps for window frames. People passed through here and like vultures picking over carrion took whatever they could loot—beds, the refrigerator, wall tiles, roof tiles, roof beams. They stripped the house to the bare bone, until nothing was left but the concrete. It would have been better if she had spent the night in the woods, she would have felt less endangered by animals there than she does by people here. Their menacing presence can still be felt in the house. This devastation is the work of human hands. Just like the death of the new-born infant at the hands of a woman who was supposed to be his grandmother. Strong peasant hands used to digging potatoes, milking cows and working in the field and around the house. Hands that know how to light a fire, make bread, wash the laundry. Hands that are good for children, trustworthy, protective. That night those hands had first assisted in the birth of the child, and then tightly tied a scarf around its neck . . .

S. looks for some sort of justification for the woman's act. War, the war made her do it. But those who started the war and led the woman to murder the child have the same excuse. If everyone has the same excuse, that they are forced to kill because there is a war on . . . is one really utterly deprived of all choice in war?

S. does not condemn the woman. She learned in the camp that people are weak and that it is not good for them to be confronted with temptation. The tiny dead body in the black head-scarf is the saddest sight S. can remember. That cold night in the ruins of the house, the image enters her dream and she knows that she will never be free of it again. The image of the little black bundle in the woman's hands is imprinted on her memory forever, the image of a woman sacrificing a child to the war because the war is stronger than both she and the child.

Sorrow pervades her very bones, there to remain like gout. Foreboding keeps her awake for the rest of the night. What would she do if she were pregnant? She thinks of the girl's mother and her adept hands. Yes, it's better this way . . .

She is afraid. This time the fear comes not from an outside threat, from the surrounding darkness, but from inside her, she can feel it in the wild beating of her heart, in the tight ball of her stomach, in her dry throat and the clammy palms of her hands. There is no where to escape from this fear, she can only suppress it deeper inside her.

I suppressed the foreboding. I knew that I must not think about it, the simple logic of survival prescribed it so.

Refugee camp, Zagreb

NOVEMBER 1992

They never actually get to see Zagreb, just the city lights rushing past the fogged-up windows. The buses to which they were transferred at the Bosnian-Croatian border stop somewhere at the edge of the city, in a field dotted with shacks. Laundry is hanging out on a line running between the shacks. This again is a camp, a transit camp for refugees. But it is not encircled by barbed wire and it does not have guards.

A sign on one of the shacks says: ADMINISTRATION. Newcomers wait there to be registered. The man sitting in the small office is tired, his questions are short. There are so many refugees, they keep arriving, giving him no respite from the huge amount of information about human misery which he meticulously writes down. He explains to them that this is merely temporary accommodation and he assigns them to the shacks. The majority sign up to go to another country. Or, if they are lucky enough, they have relatives to go to. Another country? The women look at each other in bewilderment at such news. What other country? They do not yet understand that they are now people without a country. Even S. has not thought about it and now she turns around, stunned.

The man asks her if she has any relatives in Croatia. S.

gives him the name of a distant cousin on her father's side. She has not seen her in a long time; who knows whether the woman will even remember her. She feels as if the ground is slipping from under her feet. She can be sure of nothing any more, not that the cousin will recognise her, not that she has a cousin, not even that she is the same person who once long ago sat in the lap of that same cousin as she cooed at her and sang her a little song she remembers to this day: *Silent night, my darling is asleep* . . . The sudden feeling of insecurity is like losing her balance and S. has to hold on to the table so as not to collapse. Now she is being asked to establish an urgent link with her past as if nothing has happened in the meantime, as if the thread has not been broken. For a moment S. cannot remember either the cousin's name or her face. I don't know how I would find her, she barely manages to say. Leave that to us, says the man kindly. His voice helps her to pull herself together.

Six iron bunk-beds. A wood-burning stove. A table. A woman with a white kerchief on her head tells S. her name, offers her tea and bread and shows her a free bed. A man sitting next to the stove is turning the pages of a sports paper. He has only one leg, he is the father of the family. Their three children are sitting on the bed with their hands on their laps. They are absolutely quiet. Lying on the other bed is an elderly woman, the man's mother. She looks as if she is asleep. She is sick, explains the woman, pointing at her head. They killed her two younger sons before her very eyes.

There is one more free bed. The door opens and J. walks in. They embrace as if they have not seen each other in ages. It's better that we're together, says J., we're like family now. Even she is surprised that they have been put together. Is that your sister? asks the woman. Yes, that's my very own sister, says S., glad to see a familiar face. J. did not expect them to find each other in the camp, in a cramped room, squeezed into someone else's quarters. S. tells her this is just temporary. The disabled man gives a wave of his hand. Temporary is a meaningless word. They have been here for two months already, waiting for their papers. This is where they are living, in this room, between the beds, table and stove. No, not living. Waiting. Waiting for another life while this temporary one passes them by.

The worst thing is that there is nothing to do. Time, time is killing them. The man used to work in Slovenia, on the railways. He returned to his village on the eve of the war. And then . . . He was used to working, all his life it had been work, work, work. Now idle, he does not know what to do with himself. He walks around the camp with the help of crutches. He knows some of the people. They talk over coffee and cigarettes. There is no shortage of either. They smoke, drink coffee, talk, there is nothing else to do.

They tell S. about their two houses, how big they were (the roof is four-sided, as if that is supposed to mean anything to S.). And the barn, the tractor, the thresher . . . They carefully enumerate their possessions and animals, as if this inventory of a bygone life will confirm that they did once live, exist. Their life cannot be expressed in any way other than by the size of their land, the number of cattle, machines. The children add: the television and the washing machine. They say it proudly. And then the shooting started. The house was going up in flames and they ran. The woods . . . camp . . . a nightmare. There is nothing more to add. True, they are alive, but without the house, without the land, without the animals they are utterly lost.

She has heard so many stories like this in the camp, they all sound the same. And then the astonishment. The constant astonishment that all this misery should have happened to them, why to them? As if they simply cannot pull themselves out of this state where they are caught between reconciling themselves to events and astonishment. Listening to them, S. sometimes feels that these people are still back in their village, watching their houses burn and their neighbours leading their children away. And they cannot believe it, they still think it is just a bad dream.

She acquired her coat through the Red Cross. It is big, black and comfortable. The sleeves are too long and she has to roll them up. The coat keeps her warm. She submerges herself into the smell of the coarse woollen fabric. Musty. Somebody's unaired wardrobe. If only she could stand in front of her own wardrobe now and take her own coat out. It would smell of last year's winter fog, of roasted chestnuts, of lavender which she brings back from her summer vacation every year. Belongings do help you to recognise yourself . . .

Here, in the camp, she could tell any old story, these people would have no choice but to believe her. That is not to say that refugee women like her lie, merely that they are uprooted. Their stories barely mean anything even to themselves now. No one listens to them, which is almost like not existing at all.

S. knows that she is now a refugee but she still does not know what that means exactly. How many other people's shoes and coats, how much more waiting. She still does not know that this waiting is what keeps her going, that there is no other thread connecting the moments and holding them together than this waiting for lunch, for dinner, for their documents, for approval, for news of their families, for the bus, for their departure, for their return. That is why even this camp, while not surrounded by barbed wire, is terrible. They are all waiting for something and that is what their life consists of. A refugee is someone who has been expelled from somewhere but does not go anywhere because they have nowhere to go. S. feels that she is now actually existing between two places, in a state of anticipation, in transit between the one and the other. Neither of these places is home. S. is only now becoming accustomed to the fact that this feeling of the transitory is her new situation.

But what if this life caught in the winds is all that she has left, S. wonders as she dons her new coat.

She finds it strange to be in town after everything that has happened. The main city square offers S. a sight that makes it hard for her not to burst out laughing. She feels as if she is looking at a long-forgotten but familiar sight, or as if she has stepped into a Technicolor movie. Trams running; people walking into stores and coming out with their arms full; the store windows all lit up, lovely neon signs saying: *Vartex, Naprijed, Nama, Bata, Zagrebacka banka*. High above is the flashing *Coca Cola* sign. The department store has the latest winter fashions in its windows and a shiny brown fur coat. The tall pine trees are decorated with colourful little lights. The city is already preparing for the holidays.

Here it is as if nothing has happened. Two street cleaners in orange uniforms are sweeping the tram station. They are gathering up the cigarette butts and tram tickets into a trash-can on wheels. Perhaps the war has a different face in this city. It is a face S. does not recognise. All she sees are two parallel realities: here street cleaners collect garbage, while somewhere else the collection is of pieces of human bodies. It strikes her as unhealthy to move between these two realities because then neither appears credible any more, as if both are merely her own projections.

S. walks carefully, her shoulders hunched, as if afraid

someone will stop her, shout halt, single her out, issue an order. Her movements are both stiff and hesitant at the same time. The fact that she was born and bred in a city with trams and stores and neon signs is of no help to her. That was all too long ago. She has forgotten how to walk among people who are going about their business and paying her not the slightest bit of attention.

She exchanges one hundred German marks in the exchange office. The teller does not ask her for her papers or where she comes from, she simply hands her the money. She does not have to show her yellow refugee card the way she does when she enters a bus or tram. So, when changing money, at least, she is not a refugee. Walking out of the exchange office, she feels genuine relief for the first time since she left the camp.

J., too, has changed some German marks. After so long, she is holding money in her hand which she can do with what she will. They now find this strange, they have almost forgotten about money. Nearby is a pastry shop, done up in pink marble. S. hesitates, finally walks in and orders chestnut puree with whipped cream and a cream cake. J. opts for a baklava, although she does not think it is the real thing.

The young man taking the order gives no sign that he has noticed anything different about the two of them. He lays the cakes carefully on their plates and, smiling, hands them to the two women. Please, he says. The word upsets S. Like the sight of the street cleaner in the square. She cannot remember the last time she heard the word 'please'. The lost word from another life brings her back to reality. The fact that here the word 'please' is in plain everyday use makes S. feel even more of a stranger.

The chestnut puree is dry and tasteless. S. has trouble swallowing it, as if being forced to do it. That comes from the feeling that neither she nor J. belong in this marble-decorated cake shop, among the people ordering ice cream. And as if that is not enough, they proceed to ask for whipped cream and chocolate topping. Watching, S. again feels unreal. Not so long ago she was buying ice cream herself, but that is not so simple any more.

She tries a baklava. With the very first bite she is five years old again. It is Sunday afternoon, she is with her parents taking a stroll through town, drinking ice-cold lemonade and eating a baklava which is glittering golden in the sunshine. She can smell the linden trees. Her mother says, be careful how you eat that baklava, don't get your dress dirty. Her sister holds her hand out from the stroller and says give, give . . . The pain in her chest takes her breath away. Her face is wet. She seeks solace in the quivering yellow cream cake.

She takes a deep breath, she needs air. They are walking down a wide, illuminated street where trams are passing by, people are jostling each other, and the sound of music is coming from a coffee bar. Like a child, J. stops in front of every store window. She is a village girl and perhaps has never been to such a big city before. Eighteen years old, she has graduated from a vocational school. She is wearing jeans and a leather jacket. Nothing on her betrays her stay in the camp, in the 'women's room'. She looks like any other city girl. The only thing that gives her away is her fascination with the shoe stores, cosmetic stores and shops displaying elegant evening gowns. Her eyes are starving for beautiful things and she looks at them as if she wants to assure herself that they will not disappear the moment she blinks. Soon J. will forget the camp, thinks S., looking at the girl. As she walks down the street, stopping at each window, she is no longer the person she was in the 'women's room', withdrawn and timid. One day she will don a beautiful new dress and new pair of shoes and will forget everything. S. sees in her demeanour, in her genuine surrender to the city, that J. is already forgetting and she thinks it is good that at least someone can adjust to this change so quickly.

They enter the cosmetics store and S. buys her red nail polish. She remembers how one evening, as J. was leaving with a soldier, she had looked back at the room. She had turned around and looked at them so sadly, as if certain that she would never come back to them again. Coming out of the store, S. tells her that everything that happened to them was just a bad dream and that she should forget that dream because now she is free. Later, on the bus to the outskirts of town, J. says reproachfully: why did you say that? She does not pronounce the word 'camp', she does not mention anything connected with her experience in the camp.

Soon she will not be able to talk to anyone about life in the camp, rape will no longer be mentioned, as if it had never happened. There will always be talk of the camps, the torture, the executions and so on. And the women will listen with their lips sealed. But the suspicion will remain. S. senses suspicion even in the looks that follow her around the refugee camp, in the queue for lunch, for bread, for papers. As if people are wondering: what sort of things has this woman been through? The women think such things about each other, they look at each other with the same question in their eyes. But they do not talk about it. They keep silent.

In this, S. is no exception. She too looks at the other women, trying to guess. From their eyes, from the expression on their face, from their gestures. Every woman who comes out of the camp seems to be under suspicion of having been raped. And still they keep silent. Do they think that this conspiracy of silence can conceal their shame, defend their honour? Or is it that their experience is not something one can share with others, not even with those who have gone through the same thing themselves? Silence protects us, but it also protects the rapists, thinks S., uncertain whether she herself would be prepared to talk about it.

S. frequently has dizzy spells. At first they do not worry her, she thinks they must be due to anaemia and being generally rundown. One morning she faints while waiting in line for bread and someone from management calls for first aid.

The examining doctor knows that S. has come from a refugee camp. A woman of about forty with cropped short grey hair, she is serious and does not say much. She takes S.'s blood pressure and shakes her head. Her hand is warm and strong, with short clipped nails. S. has low blood pressure, says the doctor. S. tells her about her dizzy spells, but with no headaches, she just suddenly feels dizzy, as if she is about to faint. The nurse takes a blood sample, the doctor writes in her file.

When was your last period? In May, says S., she does not know the exact date.

The doctor looks at her closely, searchingly. She has round eyes with tiny crow's feet which betray the fact that she is older than she appears at first glance. S. is afraid of the look in the doctor's eyes. She does not feel ready yet to face what the doctor is about to tell her at any minute. But the doctor simply says: do you know what month this is? November, replies S. Her words speak for themselves, but she still fends off the thought that this means she is pregnant. She feels herself frantically warding it off, and her entire body going rigid. No, she says quite calmly, that is simply impossible.

The doctor sees her despair and says that there is nothing more she has to tell her. She consoles S. by saying that hers is a normal reaction, that every person not only has psychological but also physiological mechanisms to protect them in extraordinary situations. Gently, the doctor takes her hand and tells her to come along and they will check. She moves decisively and quickly. S. surrenders herself to her, she feels there is no way out. She is utterly helpless, like a child. The old fear is now surfacing and S. knows that she is pregnant, just as she knows that she is alive and breathing. She has not a trace of doubt any more; her sentence was decided long ago and it now remains for her to face it. There is nothing left but for the doctor to read the sentence aloud. S. clenches her fists. Her nails dig into the palms of her hands.

Everything happens in accelerated motion. At the end of the corridor is another clinic. A young woman gynaecologist is there who will take her in for an examination immediately.

The doctor is careful. S. barely feels the woman's fingers inside her. Gently, the doctor presses her stomach and asks if it hurts. Her office smells of disinfectant, of rubber sheets, of alcohol. On the other side of the milky windowpane it is a winter's day. Nurses pushing food trolleys pass along the corridor, the smell of watery hospital soup trailing behind them. S. shuts her eyes but has nowhere to run.

She cannot read the doctor's face. The doctor tells her to sit down, which S. takes as a bad omen. The doctor folds her hands on the table, as if in prayer. Five months, she says, you are five months pregnant. But that's impossible, S. says again, perhaps just to say something, to hear the sound of her own voice, to know she is alive. And at the same time, she hates herself for that sentence. The last thing she remembers is hitting her head, the sound of it reverberating through her body.

She is in a hospital bed. The nun is changing the bandage on her head. Obviously, she hit her head on the table's edge and gashed her forehead. Her whole body is on fire. The nun touches her forehead. You've got a fever, she says in a worried voice, handing her a thermometer.

Her body lies in the bed like an inanimate object, an emptied bellow or shopping bag. Nothing has changed with her departure from the camp. Her body is still in their power, even more so now. Only now does S. understand that a woman's body never really belongs to the woman. It belongs to others—to the man, the children, the family. And in wartime to soldiers. Five months. A distant and remote verdict has condemned her to this condition from which there is no escape. S. feels as if someone has returned her to the camp, to the 'women's room'. She has been betrayed. This is war, inside her, in her own womb. And they are winning . . .

At day's end J. appears. She is upset, nervous. She takes two tangerines from the pocket of her leather coat and places them on the night table. The bright orange fruit is cold and fragrant. S. takes one and peels it. J.'s hand on her forehead is cold too. S. tells her she is not sick. It is far worse than that. I'm pregnant, she says. Five months pregnant. For the first time anxiety shows on J.'s face. That's not a child, that's a disease inside you, she says. S. knows that J. is thinking of herself, that she cannot bear the thought that she too is probably pregnant and that it is too late for an abortion.

S.'s first thought is the death of this being inside her womb. But when you have been through a camp, then death is no longer something vague and remote. Death is individuals, every death has a name. It is A.'s battered body, it is the stench from the wheelie bins that permeates the room for days until you think it will drive you mad, it is the men digging their own graves, the trucks carrying away the corpses, the poison E. swallowed, her dead daughter, the new-born infant that never lived to draw its first breath.

It is difficult for her to imagine that this being inside her is already alive, that it is moving and sucking its thumb, like in the photographs she once saw in a magazine. It would be best if it were stillborn. Its death would then be something natural. What sort of a future is there for a being conceived by force, in hatred, in the midst of war? It is best for it not to see the light of day. Now for the first time she understands the mother of the girl who gave birth, and the calmness of her look when the child did not cry.

The first doctor who examined her comes in and tells her that she need not agonise because it is too late for an abortion. There is a solution, however: the child can be given up for adoption. Just another four months to get through, she says. She tells her that she is not the only one, that there are many women who have come from camps and are in the same situation. She asks her no details.

Her words calm S. down, who sees that she is trying to ease the situation for her. The doctor hugs her, her firm body smelling of a floral scent. Like Mama, S. thinks. She allows herself no more than a second to picture her, her shoulders, dark hair, the smell of her hand as it stroked her face . . .

She spends a few days in the hospital. Finally she walks down the steep hill away from the hospital. It is a grey and wet morning, the cold permeates her clothes. She is alone, utterly alone, carrying this burden inside her.

The tram rumbles along to the last station. It is increasingly empty. In the end she finds herself sitting alone, watching the houses, people, trees slip past the window. S. contemplates how her own life is slipping away from her, how her life is nothing other than this slipping away.

For the first time she feels a weight in her belly. It is there, at the very bottom, like a little piece of lead. A tumour which will grow and spread and become increasingly visible.

Still, I quickly reconciled myself to the fact that I would be carrying this burden for several more months and would then give the child up for adoption. I renounced the child in advance. As if I were a mere receptacle, temporarily housing it, like a rent-a-womb.

S. can no longer avoid the thought that this is a child inside her, but she finds it easier after having made her decision because it is no longer her child. Within a short period of time she had made the mental leap from despair to some sort of relief because, just as the doctor said, there is, after all, a solution. She will rid herself of the burden, it is merely a matter of time.

She does not think about the father. Any one of the soldiers could be the father, it is of no concern to her. That even surprises S. herself. Not so much the fact that she does not wonder which of all those soldiers might be the child's father, but her own indifference. Indeed, she cannot imagine one father, only fathers.

Returning to the shack from the hospital she is greeted by the same smell of dampness, the steaming laundry, the grandmother twitching restlessly in her sleep, the quiet children. But for S., nothing is the same any more. She no longer wants to wait in the camp, watching her stomach grow, watching others watch it grow. She is becoming increasingly impatient. She wants to leave, leave for anywhere, just so long as she does not have to stay in this camp, in the compound with its stench of poverty, among peasants who do not know what to do with their time, with their hands, with themselves. She finds their endless conversations about their land, homes, cattle unbearable, but there is no place in the camp where she can be alone with herself. It is as if these people do not know of such solitude, or are afraid of it. S. realises that she has nothing in common with them, other than the war and the waiting.

J. is leaving for Slovenia. She doesn't know anything about her father but has an uncle there who has agreed to take her in. On departure, she shows S. the little bottle of nail polish and says that she is not yet free, that she is keeping it for better times. She too is pregnant. When she has the child, over there in Slovenia, she will give it up for adoption. The child will become a little Slovene and she will try to forget everything. And perhaps she will succeed, she is only eighteen.

Refugee camp, Zagreb

DECEMBER 1992

Sometime in December, S. is notified that they have found her cousin. She has not seen her in years. The last time was when B. visited them in Sarajevo with her husband and two children. S. remembers that they had just bought a new car and that the children kept pointing at it from the balcony, its blue colour making it easy to recognise in the parking lot. She wore a lot of make-up, was loud and brandished her arms when talking. Sometime later, she told them that she was getting divorced.

She comes for S. in the early evening, after work. Standing hesitantly at the door of their shack, her head is bowed as gusts of icy wind enter the room. S. looks at her, confused. Is that really her father's cousin, the same woman she remembers? Her face looks ashen now, drained. Her hair is dyed red, but she has not been to the hairdresser in a long time, because her parting clearly shows the grey in the glare of the light bulb. She is wearing an out-of-fashion coat which smells of mothballs. As they rattle along in the tram to New Zagreb, S. notices a gold ring with a blue stone on her left hand. The stone loses its shine under the neon light, as if it were a piece of plastic.

B. lives in a two-room apartment in one of those huge buildings near the river, which glows at night like a space station. You can smell the pie already on the staircase, her daughter N. is just taking it out of the oven. She is a student already, a law student. Her complexion is pale and her hair dark and when she smiles she looks like her mother, the way S. remembers her from childhood, from the family lunches and outings, before she married that car mechanic from the Bosnian provinces who had earned some money in Germany and then moved the family to Zagreb. B. works as a cashier in a supermarket, supporting the three of them. Still, S. sees that the girl is wearing brand new, and not exactly cheap, shoes. Perhaps B. notices the look she gives them. She says that at least the children are good, they are good at school, which is a consolation. Later they sit at the low table in the living room, drinking coffee. They take sips as small as the little white porcelain cups they are drinking from.

B. keeps pressing on S. her cherry preserves. S. does not dare refuse. This excessive attention makes her uncomfortable. B. says she has heard what happened to S.'s parents. She talks about it in general terms, saying: what can you do, it was fate. S. wishes she could just get up, she cannot listen to this, she finds it unbearable that somebody else should be talking about her family. But something stops her from doing anything and she remains seated. She takes some more cherry preserve. She feels sick to her stomach.

But fate may not be a bad word for something as dreadful as her family's disappearance and the uncertainty that is now her life, she thinks in consolation. What could B. say to her? How could she console her? It is best not to listen to her any more. She drinks her water and through the thick bottom of the glass sees a magnified ivy leaf on the table, its tiny veins holding some sort of whitish fluid. She retreats from this room, from herself. Immediately she feels better.

Even before this meeting, S. had thought that she might

move in with her. But suddenly she is no longer sure that this is what she wants. B. shows her the apartment, the room where she sleeps with her daughter, and the other room, her son's. She says there is space in the living room for a folding bed. S. looks around her: a table, two chairs, two bulky armchairs with brownish plastic covers, a television set, a dark cupboard covering the entire wall and making the room look even smaller. Now you have no reason to be in that awful place any more, says B. She clasps S.'s hand on her knee, squeezing it gently, as if wishing to convince her of this. Come and stay with us, her daughter adds, leaning her head on S.'s shoulder. The girl's touch sends a flow of warmth through her body and S. lets herself indulge in this agreeable feeling, this feeling of home.

S. is certain that both of them would take her in, that they have already discussed this possibility before she came to see them. If it were just her, perhaps she might move in with them, nestle in between mother and daughter and wait for the spring. But how can she tell them that she is pregnant? Perhaps they have guessed already, stories of what happened to women in the camps have already spread, they are bound to have read them in the papers. No, S. cannot do that to them. Especially as she does not know how long she may be staying in Zagreb. Until the war is over? Until she can go back to Sarajevo? She knows that for the rest of her life she will remember their invitation as something warm and kind and that is quite sufficient.

B. does not tell her everything either, at least not explicitly. She says her son could be drafted into the Croatian army at any time. Her unstated fear hovers between them, between the coffee cups and plates of preserves, between the water glasses and spoons, in the look she exchanges with her daughter. She dare not say that she does not want her son to be sent into combat. She cannot utter that in front of S. Perhaps she even thinks that S. reproaches her for not having sent her son to fight in Bosnia. But for S. her words are enough in themselves, she has learned to respect other people's fears. She consoles B., saying that he has not been drafted yet, and perhaps he will not be, he is a student. B.'s face lights up.

At the door, she tells them that she has applied to go to Sweden. Why Sweden? N. asks. Just because it is very far away from all this, replies S.

The ice at the edge of the pavement is turning thicker and dirtier. A black film of smog is sticking to the surface. S. is urgently summoned to the office. The news is brought to her one morning by R., the only man in their room apart from his little boy, who is about five or six years old. R. goes to the office every day to see what is happening with his papers, as he tells his wife. They have signed up to go to Germany, they have some distant relatives there. Many of the refugees appear to have someone in Germany. His real reason for going to the office is to kill time with the other men. S. sees them when she passes by, in the corridor, crowding in front of the office or standing in front of the door to one of the shacks. Reading newspapers that are several days old, listening to newcomers and asking them about their own relatives, friends, neighbours. Talking about politics and swearing. Every gesture they make exudes despair.

R. instinctively makes himself smaller when he enters their shack, when he enters his real life. His wife is serving lunch. The wooden spoon is scraping the bottom of the tin pot, it is the only sound in the room. Today they have bean soup and pale, over-cooked pasta. R. says: they're here! He is screeching, almost squeaking with excitement. At first S.

does not understand what he is talking about, although she sees he is addressing her. Who's here? she asks, because she is not expecting anyone. Your papers, your papers are here! Your luck has come through!, says R., practically shouting. His usual glower stretches into a smile revealing teeth stained yellow with tobacco.

S. slowly lowers her plate on to the table next to the heel of the white bread the children have been impatiently picking at. She feels the eyes of her room-mates upon her, the weight of their look. They are thinking that S. has just won the sweepstake. They are waiting. Waiting for her face to light up with a smile and give those of them staying behind in the camp hope that there is a purpose to this other life, that it is worth waiting for their papers, worth hoping. S. knows that she must not disappoint them but she is not sure that it is really joy she feels, perhaps it is more a kind of physical relief. Like climbing steep stairs and finally reaching the top. From there you have a view, and even if it is blocked by clouds, you still breathe differently, you see things differently . . .

How can she tell them that what she really feels is relief because she will no longer have to look at their brooding, worried faces or live with them in this stuffy room and eat this bland food day in and day out? No, that she must not tell them. Or show them. She forces herself to give a miserly, hesitant smile, but even that is enough for them. Weeping, the woman throws herself into S.'s arms. S. no longer knows whether this is because she is happy for S. or sorry for herself that she is not in S.'s place. Now R. is patting her on the back, the youngest child is clambering on to her lap and clapping his little hands, a strand of thin blond hair plastered with dirt to his brow. Even the child realises that something important is taking place here and that S. is in some way different from the rest of them. The spoons have been laid down, the food forgotten. A film of grey covers the soup. S. unconsciously crumbles the piece of bread in her hand.

Then R. says that they must toast the good news, the journey, a new life, and who knows what else. Ourselves, we should toast ourselves, because we have survived, but he does not say that, he does not speak the words. He pulls a bottle of brandy out from somewhere. He takes a long, thirsty swig, as if it were water. The mad old lady takes a swig too, momentarily breaking off from her unintelligible muttering, knocking back the bottle although she does not understand why there is sudden jubilation in the room. The wife also takes a drink, somewhat timidly, just a sip or two. S. drinks from the bottle too. They toast the future they all actually fear. She remembers the raised bottle, the long sip and the male face illuminated by the light bulb. And his excitement rather than her own. The strong taste of the *slivovitsa* burns her throat long afterwards.

All of us would have preferred to return to the past if only we could.

At last the document is in her hand. It is a piece of paper, confirming that her trip to Sweden has been approved. She barely glances at it, it is enough that this piece of paper allows her to leave. She is handed it by the same tired official who admitted her to the camp a month before. Crammed into the small office are a desk and two low cupboards stacked with green registration cards. On top of them is a pile of papers which look as if they are about to slip off any moment and cause an incredible mess. The Red Cross representative is there as well, Mrs P., whom they all know. She is kind and does small favours for them in town, brings them money from relatives, gets them medicine or takes their registered mail to the post office because most of the refugees feel lost in the big city. She explains that S. will not be travelling alone, she will be going with four other adults and two children. A van will take them to the airport, then a plane to Frankfurt, and on to Stockholm. In order to make sure that their documents do not get lost, she will hold on to them for the duration of the journey. S. realises that the woman says these words to everyone, that there are people who may have never left their village more than once in their lives, and for them the trip to Sweden verges on the unreal. So the woman carefully repeats the words: Frankfurt, Stockholm, documents. It is not until Mrs P. tells her that they are actually going to the Flen refugee camp outside of Stockholm that S. visibly flinches. She did not know that another camp was awaiting her there. But what on earth had she imagined? That a hotel would be waiting for her? A royal palace maybe? Of course it is a camp, what else? S. then starts enumerating: death camp, transit camp, reception camp, labour camp . . . what other kind of camps are there? Mrs P. is embarrassed, she even seems to be blushing. Don't worry, now, she says, it's not like here. S. does not ask, of course, how it could be any different; the mere knowledge that she is going there suffices to depress her. Mrs P. is now explaining that those are the rules. Refugees have to go to the reception centre first. They do not stay there long, a few months. Then they are entitled to welfare benefits, even an apartment maybe. S. clenches the piece of paper in her hand, signs some sort of registration form, and ceases to listen to the woman's every word. The story about the apartment she may be entitled to does not strike her as very convincing, not just now, not in this camp, not in this office.

Again those expectant looks! Again she feels that she owes these people a smile. Thank you, she says noncommittally to the official, to Mrs P., to the people crowding the room. The official becomes less sullen, his job suddenly seems to have a purpose. Sweden! The men in the office say nothing as they stare out the narrow, dirty window. Lucky woman, she will at least get to see Sweden and, ooh, those Swedish girls. The official removes his glasses and cleans them. His eyes are glistening. He is probably remembering the movie *Swedish Boarding School Girls* which he saw at the Lika movie theatre while still an adolescent. S. almost envies him that boyish gleam in his eye.

Gazing through the same smudged window, she sees a few hunched-over men dashing from one shack to another, sees the washing hanging on the line, almost grazing the ground, and a woman carrying a bucket of water on her head. She thinks how she has nowhere to go back to. She has reported the disappearance of her parents and sister to the Red Cross, and they promised to help her. But it will take time, they told her. She finds the camp unbearable. She will have this baby in Sweden, give it up for adoption, and then see. It must be different in Sweden, the sky at least must be bluer, otherwise her departure has no meaning. This other camp waiting for her over there is bound to be cleaner, with enough toilet paper and soap and endless amounts of hot water, and perhaps bathrooms with heating . . . Sweden must be that sort of place, where everyone is neat and clean, she has seen it on television. The mere thought of a decent bathroom with an abundance of hot water and fragrant soap is enough to nurture her wish to leave.

Since obtaining a passport (her first official document apart from her refugee card), her status in the camp has changed. As if suddenly privileged, in the kitchen she is given a better piece of chicken and a bigger portion of cabbage. People come to say goodbye. They come to the shack bearing letters for friends and relatives in Sweden, the addresses of people who may be of help to her there. An old woman has only a photograph of her grand-daughter who lives somewhere in Sweden. She has no address for her, she does not even know the name of the town where the girl is living. The old woman gives S. the frayed photograph of a smiling ten-year-old little girl with two long, dark pigtails. The girl is twenty now. Find her, implores the old woman. Helplessly, S. fingers the photograph, wondering whether to hand it back. Then she carefully packs it away with the rest of her things.

She pushes her way on to the tram. She is acting with more self-confidence, walking the city streets with a firmer, faster step, like someone who has to get somewhere, who now has a goal. But nothing is close enough to her yet, not the wet asphalt she is treading, not the cup of coffee she is holding, not the snowflakes falling on her face. As if none of this is real. Then one day she takes herself to the Cinematheque. They are showing *Out of Africa*. The cinema is practically empty. A couple are necking in the back row. A few teenagers are sitting in the middle row, their schoolbooks on their knees. The lights are dimmed.

S. goes to the movies because she has had enough of camp stories, enough of war, enough of all these tragedies. What could be further removed from her life than a romantic early-century love story set in Africa? She feels good in the darkness, she hears the rustle of a cellophane wrapper behind her and a soft sigh. She inhales the smell of the dusty plush seats. Sitting in the dark in front of the screen, the bright colours wash over her, and it is as if she can feel the sun on her skin and smell the sharp scents of the jungle. In the comfortable darkness of the cinema, the people on the screen look more real to her than she does to herself.

As she watches the pictures unfold on the screen, she remembers the moment when she felt that her life had ceased being her own, when she saw herself from the outside for the first time: it was when the young man with the gun had come for her in her apartment at the school. How long ago that was! Since then, almost everything that has happened to her has been without her own real participation. It is as if that instant she simply became a witness to her own life. While the Danish writer in her white cotton dress waits on the balcony for her departed lover's return, S. fears that her own life will never be entirely her own again. Moreover, watching the movie, she feels that everybody else's life, including this one on the screen, is more real to her than her own. As the faces of the actors flit across the screen, their words are real to her and she weeps for their suffering, just like the schoolgirls in the row behind her who are still dreaming of real life. Like when she herself was a schoolgirl, collecting pictures of film stars.

Her lap is full of tissues, she has used up an entire pack. She knows that if she does not stop sniffling, she will have nothing to wipe her nose with. So she walks out before the end of the movie. In the meantime, the winter sun has appeared outside. S. stands in front of a shoe store. The shoes are black and ugly.

Others around her are preparing for their own departures. The word 'preparing' may be an overstatement, for they have few possessions. They are chatting. They are talking about what life was like before, that is the baggage they carry. The way they talk now about their pre-war lives sounds like a fairy tale to S. Everything was great, everybody lived in peace and harmony, there were never any arguments. She could, of course, say the same thing for the neighbours in her apartment building, for her friends and fellow students at the university, but she does not see the point. Something happens, people change and you cannot recognise them any more, says the fat woman in traditional trousers, standing in line for the shower. What is worse, you cannot even recognise yourself any more, thinks S. standing in line behind her.

In the next room, one evening an old village woman with a white scarf tied over her head and across her mouth talks about her Serbian neighbour, a woman. She brought the soldiers to the old woman's house and in front of her had articles removed and loaded on to a truck. Like the others, the village woman meticulously enumerates the items: a refrigerator, two deep-freezes, a television set, a washing machine, chinaware, an electric coffee grinder, even an electric knife her son had brought her from Germany. They took the food as well—meat, potatoes, flour—she says, folding her hands. And why leave the food behind, I can even understand them taking the food, thinks S. The others in the room try to silence the old woman. They do not want to hear the same story again, it is a story they already know, they could tell a similar one themselves. They seem to be slightly tired of all this enumeration. They must sometimes be tired of the sound of their own voices, of all the unspeakable horrors amassed in the language. They will trail this dark, heavy ballast behind them wherever they go and they all feel it. Wherever they wind up, all these people will reek of the past.

She finds that it is easier for them to view their lives as a fairy tale, to remember only the best of times. An idealised, already misty past leaves scant room for the truth. But perhaps at dark moments of their lives people need to remember the good times, as if their lives had been drenched in sunlight. Perhaps that is a good thing.

Except that then we do not see our own responsibility for what happened, for the war.

We cannot go back and here we are not wanted. We have to think of the children, says K. in a practical voice. The women all nod, each of them has several children. Listening to them, a little boy says: when I grow up I'm going to kill the Serbs like this. He raises his arm and aims as if shooting someone at close range. The adults fall silent. S. knows that the boy saw soldiers kill his older brother this way. All that is missing in the child's hand is a weapon, everything else is already there. It does not matter what country he goes to, one day this boy will carry out his intention. S. walks out of the room and takes a deep breath. The air is as sharp as a knife. One generation of people in that room has already finished its life and reduced it to memories. The other will grow up with a desire for revenge. They are all like the living dead, thinks S. Suddenly there is a bitter taste in her mouth.

In a bookstore in the centre of town, S. buys a Swedish dictionary. It is actually a Swedish-Serbo-Croatian dictionary, published in 1986, before the language, like the country, was divided. The dictionary has a yellow plastic cover and is small in format. It smells of new paper. Like a textbook at the start of the school year. She spends a long time in the bookstore leafing through it, and the saleswoman is already getting impatient. Do you want to buy it or not, the woman asks point-blank. Because of the way I am dressed, thinks S., I probably look so poor that she thinks I might even be capable of stealing this cheap little book. S. finally pays and the saleswoman is left alone and content in the empty store.

S. has an espresso in the café across the road and keeps fingering the dictionary. She is excited, this is the first thing she has treated herself to. She remembered K.'s words that one should be practical and now she is somehow proud of herself for having bought a dictionary, something useful and applicable in the life that awaits her. It is like having taken out a permit for the future, her very own passport for Sweden. She is feeling restored, perhaps it is the coffee. *God dag*, she says to herself with a laugh. Good day. She says softly: house is *hem*, housewife is *huslig* . . . She has just discovered that there is something that can entertain her, she turns the pages and looks up words she finds interesting, and then she repeats them aloud. No one pays any attention to her in the bustling café.

She is curious. There is no word for 'camp' in her new little dictionary, it is too small. Or perhaps the absence of the word bespeaks the country itself, a happy land without camps. But, really, what is the Swedish word for 'camp'? Something like that must exist, after all, because that is where they are about to be housed, according to Mrs P. from the Red Cross. Perhaps it is called a reception centre? S. tries to compose the name of her destination: *antagander center* or perhaps *mottagande center*. The word for 'departure' is *avrard*. Her self-confidence seems to grow with every word she learns.

She decides that there are some words she will not learn in Swedish, she will simply omit them, skip over them. Or perhaps she will leave them behind, like the country to which such words belong. She will draw up a list of such words, one of which will certainly be *humiliation*.

At the camp, just before leaving Zagreb, S. runs into a neighbour from her apartment building in Sarajevo. F. is limping; she still has a tiny piece of shrapnel lodged in her leg which the doctors were unable to remove. She cannot sleep at night from the pain, first in one part of her body and then in another. She lived on the second floor, her apartment was not damaged. All she knows is that a refugee family has moved into it. At first F. was locked up in the washroom with several other Muslim and Croatian women from the neighbourhood. An acquaintance, a soldier in their army, saved her by getting her transferred to the other side of town. There she was wounded. She came out with a convoy of the wounded only recently.

S. does not ask her about the room. She sees in her mind's eye the former washroom on the ground floor of the high-rise building which had long ago been taken over by pensioners: the old couch with its tatty slipcovers which someone had wanted to throw out, the black-and-white television set which catches only one channel, the rickety little table and a few chairs. On the table is a box with chess pieces and an improvised ashtray made from a tin of spam. Old newspapers, the crossword puzzles already done, are stacked up in the corner.

Nor does she ask F. about her mother, whether she is alive, or where her brother is fighting. She dares not ask about her own parents and sister. These questions somehow do not cross her lips, as if she has suddenly lost the power of speech. She knows that she does not want to hear the answer. She looks at the woman's face which is now cut by two deep lines running from nose to chin. The woman's face has turned hard. It looks as if it has been carved out of stone.

F. talks about their neighbours, about the family on the eleventh floor which picked itself up and left for Serbia even before it all started; they must have known what was in the making. As for the neighbours across the way from her apartment, she says that one morning all of them, husband, wife and three children, disappeared without a trace. They were taken away, no one knows where. To the river, maybe. Maybe that's where they finished up, because there were instances of people being executed right away, says F. She says the words softly, suppressing the distress, as if fearing the echo of her own words.

Then she tells S. about Sarajevo, how it has no water or electricity. The trams are not running, the buildings have been riddled by bullets, stray dogs roam the streets. If it were not for the people you would think it was a cemetery, not a city. And people have been turning even the football stadium into a cemetery. Nothing that she has not already heard from others or seen on television, thinks S. to herself. She notices the people, be they refugees or journalists, do not know how to describe what the city looks like now. Even the pictures on television are somehow sad repetitions of themselves.

F. tells her with a smile: imagine, nobody in our building fell ill, even when temperatures dropped to minus ten! Cold and hunger are not the hardest things to bear. The worst thing is that there is no water in the bathroom, then the whole apartment stinks. A stench from which there is no escape, that is the most humiliating thing. S. does not know what to say. She laughs, as if she finds the comment about the bathroom funny, as if one can laugh at such suffering. She remembers the unbearable stench of burning corpses in the wheelie bin. She would like to tell F. a bit about her own experience of humiliation, about the types and degrees of humiliation in the camp, but she abandons the idea. Horrors should not, cannot be compared. They should not even be described. There is little hope that anyone will understand them anyway.

S. accompanies her to the bus station near the entrance to the camp. The road is deserted. As they walk side by side, F. finally tells her that she heard about S.'s parents. I didn't see them, she says, others told me. They found their bodies . . . by the river. F. cannot talk any more. She covers her face with her hands. S. feels that secret chamber opening up inside her, that last place of retreat where she can be safe and disappear. She tries to withdraw, to move away from this woman and her words. And my sister, what happened to L., she asks almost mechanically, as if asking about some acquaintance. That is all she can get past her lips. F. looks at her and then embraces her. She does not answer. She does not console her. She knows that she cannot console her. S. turns away as if about to leave, but F. grabs her by the sleeve and stops her. Leaning on her cane with one arm, she continues to embrace her with the other. It is dusk. The puddle of water around their feet is turning to ice.

S. is sick. She has been in bed for days. The nurse comes and gives her some kind of injection. A sedative probably. The psychologist comes by and tries to talk to her. But nothing comes out of S., not words, not tears. Absolutely nothing.

She remembers F. telling her that Serb acquaintances of her parents had arranged for them to be buried in the cemetery. That forces her to think about her sister. More than once she has been gripped by the crazy idea that her sister is still alive. They came for them in the early morning. It is possible that L. had spent the night with her boyfriend. Or that her parents had told her to stay in town, not to come home because they had heard that soldiers were taking away Muslim girls. And what if they had simply shoved her into the river? Or if she had tried to run away from them, and jumped by herself?

Slowly she realises that it is futile to hope that L. is alive. Bury them, she should bury them inside her, bid them farewell before leaving this place. She cannot travel to the faraway north with unburied corpses, uncertainty, trepidation, futile hope . . . Lying in bed, the covers pulled over her face, before falling asleep she thinks how it would be better if only she could cry. Like when she was a child and would scrape her knee. She would bury her head in her mother's lap and sob until the pain completely went away.

I just remember the wall next to the bed and the exhaustion. When I closed my eyes I could see my parents lying still on the riverbank. So I kept my eyes open. I looked at the wall until I went completely numb.

She does not want to spend her last evening in the room. She decides to visit cousin B. in New Zagreb; it will be a kind of leave-taking of her family. The tram is long in coming and, stamping her feet at the station, the grey light of the street lamp makes her colder still. She glances at the litter basket full of trash, at the heap of cigarette butts under her feet, at the nearby telephone booth and its solitary wire poking out. Even the new Plexiglas roof of the tram station has already been smashed. Later, walking up to the front door of the building she sees that the staircase is steeped in darkness because the light bulb is not working. She sees only ugly things, she is no longer capable of seeing anything else.

B. is in her housecoat, her pyjamas showing underneath, and somehow this softens her, a cosy sight that S. has not seen in so long. B. makes her a linden tea to warm her up, adding a spoonful of honey and a dash of milk. The tea is pinkish and fragrant. S. picks up the cup with both hands, closes her eyes and inhales the familiar smell. It makes her feel good.

A variety show with lots of singing is on television and every other song is about Croatia. B. tells her that their people at work are being sacked and that she is afraid they will sack her as well, because she is Bosnian. She does not say Muslim, but Bosnian. Sitting on the couch, knitting, her needles are so quick they seem to have a life of their own. S. inquires about her son. The only sound heard in the silence of the room is the clicking of the metal needles. B. puts down her knitting and closes her eyes. They took him . . . into the Croatian army . . . I don't know, I don't know anything. The young songstress on the television opens wide her painted mouth and sings ye-ye-ye.

Framed family photographs are displayed on the shelf. One of them is of a smiling boy in short pants, now a soldier fighting at the front. Who knows what he is fighting for. His mother is sitting in Zagreb, lost, tomorrow she may lose both her job and her apartment. S. hugs her, consoles her, everything will be all right, nobody will touch the mother of a soldier, she tells her.

As S. leaves, B. gives her a roll and cheese, wrapped in aluminium foil, to have for the journey. The roll is still hot out of the oven. And then she says, you're lucky to be leaving this place. S. feels better after her words. As if she has left part of her burden behind here, on B.'s shelf, among the framed photographs.

On the tram she sits across from a young man with only one leg. A safety pin holds up his trouser leg. The war, he says briefly, as if apologising. Here there is no escape from horror.

Her bed awaits her with the smell of dampness. She listens to the rhythmic breathing of the children in the bed beneath her and it soothes her. There is a full moon outside. The moonlight paints the film of dust on the floor silver.

Early in the morning she once again pulls out her backpack from under her pillow and packs her things, this time without fear, with just a sense of uncertainty. She has fewer and fewer possessions and that makes her happy. That red dress again, she carries it with her now out of some sort of superstition, then the unopened photograph album, some underwear, a night gown she got from Caritas, a cosmetics bag and her precious new dictionary. She adds to her backpack the roll she was given the night before. She cannot leave food behind; perhaps she does not entirely believe that she will never go hungry again. Or she feels that she owes it to her cousin, she herself does not know the answer any more. She steals out of the room without saying goodbye.

A van is waiting in front of the office. Behind the fogged-up windows, a family with two small children and a girl have already taken their seats. They are just waiting now for Mrs P. from the Red Cross, who is coming from town in her own car. The driver, dressed in some kind of uniform, is leaning against the door, smoking. S. can see only the office shack, the rest of the camp is shrouded in a white curtain of fog. She looks at that white curtain and sees it as a threat. An unease grips her. S. anxiously thinks how the trip could be cancelled and they would have to return to the same rooms, the same beds . . . The driver assures her that the fog will lift soon. S. sees that the other passengers are edgy as well. The woman is vomiting, the driver gives her husband some old newspapers to wipe the floor in the vehicle. The van reeks of acidity. The young girl is biting her nails. They all look to S. as if they would have preferred to stay in the camp that morning rather than journey into the unknown.

Mrs P. finally arrives. Her fresh hairdo still smells of hair spray. She is wearing a long fur coat which makes her stand out from the other passengers. The man is wearing sneakers, a blue synthetic track suit and an old ski jacket. His wife is wrapped up in some kind of coat of indeterminate green colour. The girl is wearing a brightly coloured nylon windbreaker, with a woollen peasant scarf on her head. S. in her over-sized black coat does not fit in with Mrs P. either.

At the airport, they all stand together in one place and

do not budge. Mrs P. tells them not to separate. Even if they were not so badly dressed, their frightened gestures and uncertain looks would betray them as homeless. S. goes to the toilet, the girl asks if she can go with her. How long will this feeling of belonging last and does it intensify the further away you go from home?

The flush tank in the airport toilet is leaking, the seat is broken. We are still in the same world, she thinks, outside the camp but in the same world.

The plane takes off, despite the fog. S. sits by herself, enjoying the fact that she is alone, if only for a moment. She reads the instructions in the event of danger and thinks how stupid it would be for the plane to crash now, it would simply be a stupid death. The sky above the clouds is blue. The blue follows her all the way to Frankfurt, even after their plane of only a dozen passengers lands there. S. is perfectly calm, the feeling that she is floating in the heavenly skies stays with her for a long time.

She shares her roll with the others. The girl with the bitten nails gladly takes a piece, crumbs of cheese falling as she lifts it to her mouth. Later she collects the cheese from her lap and eats it. The man eats hungrily as well, licking his lips and thick moustache. There is nothing like a real roll, forget about sandwiches, he waves his hand dismissively at the nearby food stand. S. is irritated by his contempt for the sandwiches nicely stacked in the window but she knows that this is his only defence against a world he does not know. His quiet wife is no longer sick. She is sitting on the floor, silently nursing her child and dozing. When she drops off, a sliver of drool trickles out of the corner of her mouth.

S. walks over to the newspaper stand. She reads the headlines in English and German and for a moment feels like a normal passenger travelling from one country to another, rather than a refugee being transferred from one reception camp to another . . .

On the plane to Stockholm, the smiling flight attendant hands her a glass of mineral water and an aspirin, just as she requested. S. avoids looking at her, she reminds her of A. The same shiny hair, the same arched eyebrows and sweet smile. For the first time since leaving the camp in Bosnia, something reminds her of the 'women's room'. A.'s face appears before her eyes. Her departure. Her death. The headache is getting worse. She closes her eyes. Is there any escape from these images?

She is still troubled by the thought that all the while the 'women's room' existed, so did this world, with its regularly flying planes and smiling flight attendants. The girl has no idea of what is on S.'s mind and brings her a mint chocolate. Indeed, why not? To suppress the scream with chocolate. The tang of mint on her tongue. She recalls having read somewhere that chocolate is good for depression.

The man sitting next to her is wearing a grey business suit. He is reading the sports page of some German newspaper. His thin, soignée wife is leafing through a fashion magazine. They do not talk to each other. Silent, the two of them look like part and parcel of the aircraft's decor, their appearance utterly in tune with the grey of the seats, carpet and plastic glasses. S. is getting accustomed to a world where no one asks her any questions. She does not want to be any different from these people, submerged in their disinterested, perfectly functioning world. War? What war?

Stockholm

DECEMBER 1992

By around four o'clock in the afternoon, it is already dark in Stockholm. The icy wind stings her face and eyes. Her lungs hurt when she inhales the cold air. The dark, crystal sky, the cold, the neon lamps casting their orange light on to the asphalt, these are the first images she has of the country she intends to live in from now on.

The small group hangs together, they are all still together. They head for the airport bus like some sort of school excursion group. They take the back seats, just to be able to sit next to each other. They hold their bags on their knees rather than place them on the luggage rack. These bags with clothes received from Caritas are their only certainty, the only thing they are sure of. The girl next to her wraps her arms around her small sports bag and rests her head on the cold plastic bearing the Adidas logo.

Two women are waiting for them. At the exit S. immediately notices a face framed by a crop of dark hair. It looks vaguely familiar. The striking eyes and mole on the cheek . . . she tells herself it is impossible. She lets her eyes glide across this face in the crowd. Then she hears a voice, a female voice. It is calling her by name. She is certain now. It is G., the third bench next to the wall. Primary school. She knows her resonant voice, she used to sing in the choir and recite at all school events. Her father worked abroad somewhere and then in the mid-eighties G. and her mother left as well. She turns around. She still cannot believe it, even though there is no doubt left. She has stepped out of a school photograph from a 1975 excursion to Tjentište. G. had long hair at the time. How can S. be running into her here at the airport? She stops and looks at her for a moment, still unsure. But G. walks up to her, touches her, hugs her, making sure. For her, too, S. has stepped out of the school photograph. G. welcomes refugee groups at the airport, translates for them, sees them settled in the camp, helps them find their feet. My biggest fear is that I will see among the refugees somebody I know, she tells her. I find it harder when I come across a familiar face, when I know where the person comes from, because we grew up together. S. looks closely at her face, she is already turning grey and has crow's feet around her eyes. Who knows how G. sees her. Every time G. smiles, the mole on her cheek moves.

As the bus drives off, G. quickly makes a decision. She tells S. that she will not leave her at the Flen reception centre with the others. She will take her home with her. Her voice sounds firm as she talks to the other woman who welcomed them. She assures her, explains to her. The older woman in the white jacket shakes her head. She twists the rough woollen gloves she is holding, she seems somewhat hesitant. G. goes on talking in a low voice. The other woman nods her head, as if finally agreeing: all right, she can go, but it is your responsibility, you know the rules . . .

The bus speeds down the wet highway. All the way she is followed by that orange light which spills on to the snow, a light she cannot accustom herself to. They are surrounded by woods, dense and impenetrable as a wall.

G. now explains to S. that she did the same thing two

months earlier with another refugee. And that it is, of course, against the rules, but they can come to an arrangement. S. listens to her and looks at Mrs P. The woman in the white jacket is explaining the situation to her. Mrs P. turns around perturbed, it is evident that she is not pleased. She keeps shifting in her seat. She clutches her hand luggage. She casts a look at S., perhaps expecting her help. Perhaps she thinks she is losing control of the situation, which is not good. It could make her lose her job. On the other hand, her task is only to bring the refugees to Stockholm, or wherever it is they are going. For all intents and purposes they are now in the hands of the Swedes. All this flashes through Mrs P.'s mind even before G. tells her that she need not worry because she will arrange all the formalities concerning S.'s stay tomorrow. She has nothing to do with the two women's latest decision. That clearly calms her down. While they are talking, S. looks at their reflection in the bus window. Their faces are pale and flat, like paper cuttings.

Mrs P. turns around and calls out to her, somewhat angrily, you were lucky. Lucky? She is talking about being lucky? S. is tired of the chain of coincidences, of the sudden turnabouts in life, of the capriciousness of her situation which anyone can overturn. In the bus, in the office, the camp, her apartment. As if still she does not exist.

At the last bus stop they part as if they are a real family. They kiss, hug, weep. They keep saying goodbye and good luck. As she kisses her, the girl's nose is running but her fear of the unknown is such that she fails to notice it and smears it all over her face. S. is grateful to G. not to be travelling on with them, if nothing else at least she will free herself of that feeling of group belonging. Albeit an unwanted group, even though language, origin and memories are also what tie her to G. This will all now resurface from the shallow grave in which S. tried to bury her past. Fortunately, they must say their farewells quickly because the wind is chilling their bones and they have to travel on, to Flen. It is still daytime, although it is already pitch black outside, as dark as night. Soon they are all swallowed up by the darkness, along with Mrs P., whose fur glistens as they move off and out of sight.

The kitchen smells of stuffed cabbage. G. laughs at her disbelief. Naturally, her mother made her a pot of stuffed cabbage for the weekend. At the market here you can get heads of pickled cabbage, home-made bacon, hot peppers, even *Vegeta* seasoning. She says there is a stand run by a Serbian family, they even have real Srem sausages. G. tells her all this with genuine enthusiasm. Anyway, do you even remember the last time you ate stuffed cabbage, she asks her.

Yes, S. does remember, it was last winter, almost exactly a year ago. On New Year's Eve when they were seeing in 1992 at a girlfriend's apartment. It would be an effort for her to have to say exactly which ethnicities her friends there that night were. Slightly tipsy, she danced with M. She remembers longingly resting her head on his shoulder, being excited by the closeness of his body. They kissed. Just before daybreak they ate stuffed cabbage.

The kitchen is bright and faces the courtyard. Leaning on her arm, S. looks around: a copper coffee pot and Turkish coffee cups are neatly lined up on the shelf. Along with them is a manual coffee grinder. An embroidered tablecloth covers the table. A copper plate hangs on the wall, just like the ones sold in the bazaar in Sarajevo. Her eyes stumble over the little red stitches on the tablecloth that open up into a rose. She feels unable to extricate herself from the past. Every single object reminds her of something she has seen before, experienced before. These objects are like obstacles, stumbling blocks which make you trip and fall. It all wounds her; S. still lacks a defence mechanism to protect her against her own bitterness, fear and sorrow. Her biggest fear is that she will start to pine for what she left behind, that she will forget why she came here. She again falls into the crack between the past and the present. She simply cannot find the bridge which will take her to the other side where she can forget everything, once and for all.

She only begins to feel better when they start talking about school, about things that happened fifteen years ago and more. This she does not feel as a threat—R., the math teacher who tweaked the students' ears when he was angry; C., the spinster music teacher; the excursion to the Sutjeska river when the two of them shared a room. G. suddenly tells her that her mother is Serbian. I wasn't even aware of it until the war, says G., and then looks down at the *sarma*. My mother was Serbian too, says S.

She sleeps for a long time, dreamlessly. She wakes up in a room with yellow curtains. The soft light traces a latticed pattern on the white carpet. G. has left on the radio and the coffee machine. A woman is singing something about love. S. is glad to be able to recognise the odd word. Remember these words, look them up in the dictionary. I have to start right away, now, she thinks to herself. She eats oatmeal with hot milk and watches the cars at the intersection. Then she goes back to bed. This first day is empty, a comfortable day without anything happening. Without thoughts. She feels as if this day has been given to her as a bonus.

Stockholm

JANUARY 1993

G. takes her to the Café Opera; crystal chandeliers hanging from the ornate ceiling, white tablecloths, elegant waiters. They sit down by the big windows that look out on to the royal palace. S. eats delicate pink salmon. The fish is so beautiful she is almost sorry to eat it. She is glad that she in no way stands out from the people around them. S. knows that she is a foreigner here, perhaps even an intruder in normal life. But at the same time she hopes that nothing bad will happen to her any more, that that is over, that these people here have no intention of hurting her just because she is not one of them.

I still want to believe that.

She is suffused with a feeling of warmth. For the first time she feels truly warm. Perhaps it is the wine. Wine reminds her of the Captain, she has not touched a drop since leaving the camp. But she does not want to think of him, remember him. She drinks some more, in long, thirsty gulps. She soon feels tipsy. She points at the plastering on the ceiling and laughs louder than she should. An old couple at the next table turn their heads towards her and smile. G. orders another bottle of strong, heavy Spanish wine. Frozen-over water gleams between the restaurant and the royal palace.

The silvery shine of the frozen water makes her feel as if she has just stepped into a northern saga . . .

They are in the bedroom. G. opens her wardrobe. She flicks through it quickly. S. sees neatly hung skirts, pants, jackets and several coats. G. is looking for something to give S., because she has been wearing nothing but the same long skirt and sweater ever since she arrived. Under the sweater she is wearing a large plaid shirt. I have so many things I never wear, says G., as if suddenly ashamed of her own urge to accumulate unnecessary things. She has her back to S., who is sitting on the bed. S. does not know how to tell her, she does not know whether G. has perhaps noticed her stomach protruding under her clothes. It already shows, she can see it herself when she is showering. Her thinness makes her tummy look even bigger. S. is not ashamed, but still it is hard for her to say it: I'm pregnant. She is afraid that G. will not understand, that she will think S. could perhaps have aborted. This way, she will think that S. wants this child.

G. pulls out of the drawer a grey pair of trousers, a sweater, top, blue dress and blouse and shoves them all at her. Try them on, she says. She lies down on the bed, propping herself up on her elbow and waits. Like a little girl trying on her mother's clothes with a friend. She shows her the mirror and says she won't look while S. is dressing. How can S. tell her she is pregnant?

S. slowly gets undressed. First the shirt, then the undershirt. Still G. does not notice anything. No, nothing. Her face is childishly bright and smiling. Now the skirt has slipped to the floor as well. S. is almost naked. You're so thin, says G., you have to eat more. Even now she does not notice. S. turns sideways and places her hands on her stomach. I'm pregnant, she says slowly, more than six months pregnant.

G.'s face changes as if a dark cloud has crossed it. She

knows that S. was in a camp, but that is all. However, even that is enough for her to realise how S. became pregnant. G. lies on the bed with her eyes closed. Without a sound or a gesture, as if shattered by the words. S. stands there, sure that G. understands. Should she put her clothes back on or try on what G. has given her? She decides to try on the dress. It is slightly wide in the waist, she says, just what I need. G. is silent, she does not look at her.

Several days have elapsed. S. tells her her decision to give the child up for adoption as soon as it is born. G. is not surprised, she simply says that she will help her, she has already helped another woman who was imprisoned in a hotel outside of Sarajevo. She interpreted during her talks with the social worker and the psychologist. The woman is still at the Flen reception centre, waiting to give birth. Don't worry, the authorities here will abide by your decision. If that is what you have already decided, G. adds.

S. senses a note of disapproval in her voice. Or perhaps it reflects some doubt that this is the right decision. S. is hurt by her strange comment. Does G. think she should keep the child? She replies in almost a whisper, trying to conceal her disappointment: you don't understand . . .

Absorbed in thought, G. grinds the coffee, then she slams the spoon down on the table. I simply meant that in my opinion the child is not to blame, she explains. S. wants to tell her how strange she finds it that G. should talk about the child. As if the child already existed and was crying in the next room. How is it that she does not see the person sitting there in front of her and looking at her? Why does she talk about the innocence of the child, and not about her own innocence? Is maybe she to blame? And what is she to blame for? How to hide from the righteous who are so sure that they know what is best in such a situation? The worst thing is that they neither listen nor hear. They mean well, but they do not hear. S. sees how the kitchen light falls on G.'s face. As she talks about the child, G. leans forward, in an effort to be convincing. She looms over her like a bird.

S. quickly distances herself. She sees the kitchen, the two of them in it, the cups on the table, everything. But G.'s words can no longer touch her. S. is beyond anyone's reach, she is safe.

They fall silent. G. sees her withdraw and abstains from further conversation. S. thinks: there is no way anyone can understand me. And she withdraws still more.

Of course the *child* is not to blame, no child is to blame. But to her this is not a child, it is a burden she is carrying in her stomach. Because she has been forced to do so. It is something that is stealing her cells and reproducing, feeding on her blood, on the air that she breathes. To her it is a parasite. At night, lying on her back, she can feel it move and that disturbs her. The thrashing of a trapped animal striving for release keeps her awake. In the middle of the night she is alone with this unfamiliar hungry being residing in her womb.

It was not G.'s fault, she could not understand me. Perhaps everything still happening over there is far from understandable.

It is not until she is in her own apartment in Rinkeby that S. begins to understand what G. has done for her. She thought that G. had an obligation to her because they knew each other, because they came from the same region, because who knows why. An obligation not only to take her in rather than let her go to the camp like everybody else, but also to arrange through her friends for S. to obtain residence papers quickly, and even an apartment. She let G. spend days on the phone and on making the rounds of various offices, without ever asking whether she was tired of taking care of her. Living with her, she thought it was somehow normal.

I behaved as though everybody owed me something. Others had to correct the injustice done, those who had had the least to do with the war. I did it unconsciously, of course, but that in no way excuses it.

She eats. She cannot stop. G. buys sausages, salami, cheeses, butter, different spreads. S. puts ham, cheese, eggs, mayonnaise and pickles between two thick slices of bread. She chokes on the large bites. An hour later she is hungry again. She buys a big piece of meat and roasts it with potatoes. She bakes cakes, apple pies. She makes a full plate of oatmeal with milk and sprinkles cinnamon over it. Or rice pudding. She does not like fruit, only heavy food. She remembers a neighbour from Sarajevo who could tell from what a pregnant woman ate and from the shape of her stomach whether the baby would be a girl or a boy. It follows, then, that hers will be a boy. The thought makes her sick.

Every evening she welcomes G. with three or four different dishes and winds up eating most of them herself. One evening she is so hungry she goes down to the supermarket, buys herself a tin of fish, a baguette and a box of cookies, and washes it all down with beer. Sometimes she gets up at night, awoken by her rumbling stomach. She opens the refrigerator and takes out a slice of salami or cold piece of meat. Or a slice of bread, anything that will satiate and calm her so that she can sleep. S. knows that she is actually soothing the needs of this being growing inside her, but she is unable to defend herself against his hunger.

As the days pass her stomach grows. It is already large and very visible. She does not try to hide it any more, she no longer conceals it under layers of voluminous shirts and sweaters. She sticks her stomach out and is surprised when, on the underground or the bus, people politely stand up to give her their seat. As if she were just an ordinary pregnant woman. That is exactly how they see her, like any other pregnant woman, thinks S. bitterly. But even her bitterness is subsiding. The unwanted burden is gradually taking over, making her slower, more sluggish, more lethargic.

Bus no. 43 is crowded. A young man leans out the door and offers her his hand to help her up on to the platform. She cannot explain to everyone that this stomach of hers is only a space temporarily lent to a being she will never meet. Something like a sub-tenant—a being but not a person.

Stockholm

FEBRUARY 1993

The corridors of the Immigration Office are bright and clean. Seeing her stomach, the official invites her into the room and offers her a seat. She looks like a teenager, she has freckles and a fringe. The room is not very big, with potted plants on the window sill: camellias, ferns, tiny cacti. Her file is lying on the table in a yellow folder in front of her, right next to a pot of cyclamen with big violet flowers. While the official goes to get coffee, S. touches the leaves. They are real, not plastic. She feels better after touching them.

The woman offers her a paper cup of watery coffee. S. does not want to offend her so she drinks it. Then, together with G. she fills in the forms. S. sits in the comfortable chair, gazing at the impossibly green rubber plant in the corner. She still does not understand this country, where you can sit down in an office and get a cup of coffee, sometimes even a cookie. And where there are no crowds, there is no waiting in the corridor. Where she comes from, for every document or paper she had to wait for hours, on her feet, squeezed between the lumbering bodies of men who pushed her aside and stepped on her feet or jumped the line. The corridor's shiny walls were soiled by the waiting bodies that pressed against them. Everybody smoked, and then put their cigarette butts out on the floor with the heel of their shoe. In front of the counter you could never be sure whether you had filled out the form properly, bought enough tax stamps or brought along the right number of photographs to attach to the documents. She could never be sure of anything. How could they have taken all this? Was it because they did not know any better?

The Swedish psychologist carefully reads the Zagreb doctor's letter. G., of course, had translated it. The furniture in the room is made of metal and glass. Sitting on a white armchair, S. somehow feels uncomfortable. She gazes at a framed photograph of a man and two children and waits for the psychologist to speak. The silence is broken only by the ticking of an antique clock and the rustle of paper.

Submerged in the whiteness of the armchair, a numbness takes hold of S. The psychologist is now taking notes as G. explains the situation. Finally she turns to S. and asks her when was it that she decided not to keep the child, but she does so without looking her in the face or in the eye. S. explains. Is her decision final? Perhaps there are relatives who would be willing to accept the child, asks the psychologist. She does not raise her head from the papers. Relatives? But they are in Bosnia, says S. There is a war going on. Does she need to explain that to her as well? I am a refugee, S. adds, with no hope that this woman will understand. She again has that feeling that talking is useless. They are all kind, they will even help her, but they cannot understand her.

She holds her hands on her knees. She lowers her eyes. Suddenly the room is dark. She looks at her hands. They seem dead, quite dead. She no longer feels anything in them. S. sometimes thinks that she lost all feeling in her hands when she stepped on to the bus in front of the village school, when she had packed her things and boarded the bus. Everything became wooden to her touch. Her clothes, bread, potatoes, earth, grass, hair, cement, soap, skin. They are about to leave when S. turns around and says out of the blue: can I please change my name? I want to be somebody else. I'm tired of myself. I feel like a watermelon which is about to burst any minute. I will collapse in some street and all that will be left of me is pieces. You know, like a big, round, ripe watermelon, she says. She immediately wonders whether the psychologist has ever seen a whole watermelon. Really, how else can she explain that nothing holds her together any more? She has no centre. She is unsure when talking about herself. She is constantly plagued by a feeling of shame and guilt which keeps undermining her.

G. looks at her oddly but translates. The psychologist removes her glasses and looks her in the eye. S. has the feeling that she is seeing her for the first time. Do you think that is possible? asks the psychologist. Once again S. feels she is drowning. She forgets that she should be happy because the psychologist did not ask her awkward questions. On the contrary, it was simple. She could have fared worse.

G. squeezes her hand and says she need not worry, it all went well.

Rinkeby, Stockholm

MARCH 1993

The city authorities allocate her an apartment in a suburb of Stockholm. The apartment is in a newish building. The staircase smells of fresh paint and varnish. The large room overlooking the woods is empty but full of light. That first night S. sleeps on a mattress on the floor, in an empty apartment, in a bare room. Late at night she lies on her side and falls asleep with the smell of glue in her nostrils, a smell which gives her hope that here everything will be all right. The future smells of flooring, wood, glue and fresh plaster.

One by one, new objects start restoring S. to life. She buys her first pieces of furniture with hesitation. She sees a plain country chair in an antique store in Gamlastan. She walks by several times but does not dare walk in and buy it, even though it is not expensive. Like other refugees, the state gave S. some money with which to furnish her apartment modestly. But the chair reminds her of her grandmother's chair, the one she would bring out in front of her house in the village when spring arrived, and sit on while shelling peas or knitting. Perhaps it would be a good idea to furnish the apartment with objects which would each remind her of a person or an event. To furnish it with memories. It would suffice for her to enter a store like that and buy things that remind her of home: old glasses, a glass hound or flute-player, figurines that once stood on the chest of drawers in her parents' living room.

In a china shop S. wavers, fingering a big soup bowl and blue-ringed plates, heavy silver cutlery, octagonal brandy glasses. She even finds floral-shaped transparent glass dessert plates like the kind her mother had received as a wedding present in 1959. Standing there in the store, she suddenly has a vision of her mother lifting the lid off the bowl. An aromatic cloud of steam rises up. She scoops up the soup with a silver ladle, the yellow noodles spilling over the edge, and S. holds her plate up so that the soup does not spill on to the white Sunday tablecloth . . .

In the end she surrounds herself with completely new things, not one of which reminds her of her past life: a table and four chairs, a bookshelf. Everything is made of light wood, of fir. Then there is the blue-and-white striped two-seater couch. The room is light. Soothing and utterly Swedish. This is home to S., a place where she can be alone. In her new apartment, in this Swedish room, in her Swedish life, there is no room for a child.

Lying in bed in the mornings, S. often gazes at the sky. From the third floor she usually sees heavy clouds impaled on the tops of the nearby fir trees. The clouds sometimes hang suspended there for days, immobile. Only occasionally does a ray of sunshine pierce through this cotton mass and then she is finally dazzled by the blue she so longed for in the shack in Zagreb. The winter sky is leaden and menacing, darkness falls early. Now with each passing day the sky is getting lighter, as if the clouds are growing thin, melting from the sun above.

It is March already and the sky is clear with just a few white clouds slowly rolling from one side of the window to the other. Spring must be around the corner, though she cannot be sure exactly when spring arrives here or which flowers herald it. She bought a bouquet of red tulips in the supermarket the other day. They wilted that same evening, they must have come from a nursery. Walking down the lane in front of the house she turns around and looks for snowdrops. She wonders if there are any snowdrops in Sweden, and if they are the same snowdrops. And what about the little bouquets of violets they sell at the market in Sarajevo? Or hyacinths? S. longs for the smell of wild hyacinth. Perhaps she is longing for Sarajevo, but that is something she does not dare admit to herself.

She walks with increasing difficulty, moving awkwardly around the apartment as if it had shrunk. She keeps bumping into the doorknob or tripping over the doorstep, the chair is in her way, she can barely reach the dishes in the dishwasher. It tires her to move and she would be happiest if she could just stay in bed. Sometimes her own body is so heavy that she actually does not get out of bed. Living in the same building is a family from Bosnia who came here twenty years ago. The mother comes over in her dressing gown bearing a pot of soup and a piece of meat and spoon-feeds her. Soon you will be rid of your misery, she consoles her.

She is due to give birth soon, any day now. But she has no patience left, she is becoming more and more tetchy. She is afraid of giving birth. She simply cannot bear the monstrous shape she has become any more. Her hands and legs are swollen, sometimes she cannot even make a fist. When she lies down on pillows she sees her pointed belly with its bulging navel and once small breasts now enlarged like risen dough. She cannot recognise any of it and it upsets her. She is standing in the kitchen, boiling potatoes. Turning around to reach for the salt, she sees her reflection in the hall mirror. And she is taken aback because she sees this strange woman who lives here in the apartment with her. This fat, awkward companion, her double.

One morning the clouds are white and thin, like sheets billowing in the spring breeze. The sky is so blue that after a few days of exhaustion S. resolutely gets up out of bed, has her shower and makes herself breakfast. A towel is still wrapped around her head. The smell of real Turkish coffee fills the kitchen. She spreads honey on a slice of home-made bread given to her by her neighbour the night before, and as she lowers herself on to the kitchen chair she feels a stab deep inside her stomach. At first it is not real pain, more like a kind of unpleasant pressure. S. squirms on the chair. She realises it is time and that this is the first gentle sign, heralding labour pains. But she decides that she will have her breakfast in peace and quiet. That no sudden arrival is going to spoil her morning.

Then the contractions start coming closer together. S. has everything ready for the hospital. She just needs to put them into the backpack with her other things. It remains for her to telephone G. She has time to dry her hair before G. arrives. At last, she thinks, at last the day has come. She is surprised by her own calmness.

A moment after giving birth she feels something wet and sticky on her chest. It is all over. She is short of breath, breathing rapidly, still trembling from the exertion. Her legs are shaking. Somebody is wiping the sweat off her brow. She shuts her eyes. Half-asleep she hears the opening and closing of doors, the cry of a baby in another room.

And then something utterly unexpected happens: the

nurse lifts up the edge of the sheet covering her and lowers something wet and warm on to her chest—her new-born child. S. opens her eyes and cries out No, No. Or thinks she does. Perhaps only a whisper comes out of her open mouth. The nurses are busy with a woman giving birth on the other table. Not one of them pays any attention to S. She lies there paralysed. She does not dare move. Lying on her breast is a naked, still blood-stained tiny body. The creature is turned to its side. It lets out a weak sound like a cry and waves its tiny fists, then opens its eyes and looks at S. Two dark eyes stare out at her from the red, wrinkled little face with its plaster of hair.

The touch of her own warm skin soothes the little thing and it peacefully falls asleep. No one had warned her of the custom at Swedish maternity hospitals to place the new-born infant on the mother's breast immediately after it is born. The little boy lies on top of her like an unfledged bird. S. does not know whether she feels mere disgust and pity or something else as well. Lying there with this little sleeping thing on top of her, she is amazed that it does after all exist. In spite of everything, their two lives are still connected. She looks at it again, carefully this time and with less fear: he is breathing evenly, comfortably nestled on his side, listening to the rhythmic beat of her heart. His warm body warms her breasts. She feels how everything inside her is focused on the child, on the fact that this is a child, after all, not a monster. As if, by looking at this sleeping being, a deep gash opens up inside her, like a wound that will never heal. He is so tiny, so vulnerable, like a little animal that does not know what awaits it, thinks S., closing her eyes again.

Finally the nurse removes the child, wraps it in a diaper and whisks it away somewhere out of S.'s range of vision. All she can see is his little head of damp black hair. She is absolutely convinced that she will never see him again.

She wakes up in a room. Still half-asleep, she does not notice at first that a transparent Plexiglas cot has been placed next to her bed. Inside it is a baby, but S. does not recognise it. It does not even occur to her that she might find her own child here.

Karolinska Hospital, Stockholm

NIGHT OF 27–28 MARCH 1993

She gets out of bed and presses her brow against the transparent glass. The window looks out on to a park of birch trees. Further on is the sea and the cloudless light blue sky of the north. Everything here is so soothingly foreign. As if she is on another planet. Yes, this is where she will live. She will don this reality like a clean, brand new blouse. She has decided that this is how it will be. And what can stop her from doing this? She touches the cold glass with her fingers. The touch of the smooth surface on her fingertips feels good.

The baby turns its head to one side and puts its finger in its mouth. It is hungry. It sucks vigorously at its little finger. Watching it, S. no longer feels hatred or anything. Curiosity perhaps. It is no longer a part of her and now she can completely relax. She can admit to herself that it is a beautiful, healthy baby, with a nicely shaped head, forty-nine centimetres long and weighing in at 3,700 grams.

Maj is awake. She holds the baby out to her. S. signals that she does not want to take it into her arms. Maj gives her a worried look. She does not understand her rejection of the child. She does not know that there has been a simple misunderstanding. Perhaps it is the fault of the duty nurse who brought the child in; she looks young and unsure of herself.

She must have given the papers just a cursory glance. She probably cannot imagine that S. does not want the child. Why would anyone in Sweden not want a child? How wonderful it is to be born here! A vase of Japanese violets stands on the table. Clean white curtains hang from the windows. They have a large bathroom at their disposal, one for the two of them. The nurses are kind, they tiptoe in every so often to ask if the women need anything.

It would all be fine were it not for this mistake. The nurse simply put the child in the cot and undressed it, probably to show her how to change diapers and so that she can see that the child is all right. At first S. cannot believe that this child can be with her in the same room. She tries to say something, to explain to the nurse, using her one hundred words of Swedish. She cannot remember the word for 'mistake' and that irritates her. She can hear her voice tremble and her own helpless, pathetic stuttering. She realises that she is still too weak to undertake anything; she breaks into a sweat at the mere effort of saying these few words. The nurse thinks she is in pain and asks where it hurts, pointing first to her stomach and then to her head. S. goes limp. She will have to wait for the situation to resolve itself.

Yes, when the psychologist and social worker arrive the misunderstanding will be cleared up. Then they will realise the mistake, the stupid mistake they have made. She will show them the document, the letter from the psychologist describing her decision and the reasons why she cannot keep this child. They will understand that this child wound up beside her through their own mistake and that she should never have come into contact with the child. The nurse will finally take it away somewhere and S. will never see it again. She will forget what it looks like. Her body will forget it too.

Oblivion is within reach and S. expects to be able finally to sink into this state of bliss.

Meanwhile, the baby is lying in its cot beside her, perfectly quiet and devoted, as if this is its place.

She is tired. She wishes she could just fall asleep and wake up somewhere else. How often in the past year has she had this same, identical wish, to wake up somewhere else, to be somebody else . . . She tries to console herself with the thought that only another day or two separate her from freedom. If everything goes well, she will sign that last paper tomorrow. Her nightmare will be over. Perhaps she will not dream the same dream any more and like everything else the childbirth will sink into the darkness of the past. Now all she wants is to be alone. Although they do not talk, Maj bothers her. She could talk to her in English if she tried, but what would she say? There are some words she does not want to utter ever again. They are too hard. Sometimes she feels as if she has a mouth full of stones. How can she say the word 'house', when she has no more house. Or country. Or the word 'camp'. Who knows what the word would mean to Maj, probably something from the newspaper or television, or a book about World War II.

Can someone like her understand a life that has suddenly been interrupted, then started from scratch, but as if it were someone else's life? And how would she explain to Maj her decision to give the child up for adoption? What would she, from the perspective of her peaceful settled life in Sweden, think of this decision? How can you talk about war when you know that the person you are talking to cannot even conceive of such horror? It is like being deaf and having no hearing aid. She had tried to talk to G. when she was living with her. She had talked to the psychologist too, and told her that she had been raped. But her words seemed to have slid past them, as if they did not quite concern them. It would be the same with Maj.

S. says nothing. She does not respond to Maj's attempts to start up a conversation. She wants to be alone. She has had enough of forced proximity. When she thinks of all the time she has spent in a crowd—they slept in a crowd, ate in a crowd, performed bodily functions in a crowd. Now she avoids the proximity of human bodies in shops, on the bus, in the underground. She likes to walk in the meadows in her neighbourhood. Because of the close proximity of people, she goes to town only when she has to. Then she stands on the shore and looks, the city is so pretty in early spring. The sunlight refracts against the yellow and orange façades of the buildings and their reflection shimmers on the water's surface as if about to vanish any moment. Leaning on the railing of a bridge for a second, she is actually afraid that it is merely an apparition. Then she rouses herself. The city is real. The breeze carries the smell of the sea, the air is crisp and clean. She breathes. She breathes and that moment she feels good.

Unable to calm the baby boy down, Maj is now feeding it at her own breast. S. watches him slurp contentedly and suddenly she is overcome with deep sadness. His life will be determined by the way he was conceived. And by the fact that he came into this world here, rather than there. He will be adopted, he will become somebody else. Now, looking at him closely, S. thinks how unfair it is for his life to start this way. The most she can do is wish that someone gives him a better past. That would be the best gift for him, thinks S. Perhaps along with her written approval for adoption she could enclose a little letter to his future parents. In it she would tell them to construe the nicest possible past for this child, because his future will depend on it. But perhaps they would not understand such a message. She could, of course, explain it to them, tell them what she went through because of who her parents are, because of where she was born, where she wound up . . . Still, it seems to her best that the child does not take any baggage with him on his trip, that his origins remain unknown. Who his parents were, where they are from, and especially their nationality. Because when somebody comes from those regions they usually bring only misery and unhappiness with them.

Maj indicates for her to take the child into her arms. S. understands, but shakes her head. Again, Maj leaves the sleeping Britt and picks him up herself. She walks around the room with him, humming a Swedish lullaby. Now S. is satisfied, the scene completely calms her. She already imagines a big-breasted Swedish woman becoming the child's mother. She had not been entirely aware that she had just given birth to a little Swede. Soon he will have a new identity. Albeit a false one. But does that matter? What will his own new identity be like? Will her life in this foreign country, without friends and without a past, be less false than his?

Night is advancing. A lamp is burning on the little night table. The baby is still asleep. Last night the nurse came and bottle-fed him. A different nurse, the night nurse to whom Maj explained that S. is not nursing the baby, perhaps because she has no milk. S. did not enter into any explanations, she pretended to be asleep.

Maj has fallen asleep. S. looks at her long hair, at the beads of sweat on her brow and her unbuttoned shirt. How old can she be? She feels close to her in a way, they have in common the past few months of feeling a weight, of pain, and then the exertion of squeezing out the baby, the cramps, the bleeding, the exhaustion . . . There is so much she could tell her about a body that lives independently of a person's will, about the way a body can be enslaved which is known only to women. Here, life, anybody's life, seems to unfold in a different dimension, one devoid of horror. There is individual fear and individual pain. But not the all-embracing horror of war in which there is nothing to protect a woman from male cruelty. To her surprise, S. feels that she envies Maj. Tomorrow Maj will pick up her baby and leave for something familiar and safe.

Her nipples are wet with milk which keeps oozing out on its own. This is probably what is keeping her awake, this unpleasant tension. This new feeling of pain in her breasts. The wet towel. Only now does she see that the baby is dressed in a little outfit bearing the logo TILLHOR LANDSTINGET, public property. Little Britt has the same logo on her outfit, the same letters are inscribed on the sheets, the night gowns, towels and pillow-cases. But the words 'public property' on his outfit look to S. like a symbol of fate. Only just born and already he belongs to somebody else, not to himself, he does not know exactly to whom . . .

The child turns and S. sees he has uncovered himself. With a single gesture she pulls the little yellow blanket up to cover him.

She did it quite unintentionally, perhaps she is not yet fully awake. She saw that the child was uncovered and covered it, without thinking. But it is this very gesture that deprives her of sleep. She thinks about how, by virtue of this unconscious gesture, she has done something against herself. She almost touched him, and that is absolutely not to be done. She is still afraid of touching, of such unbearable closeness with the child. She still recoils from him.

The hospital is completely silent. Maj does not make a sound, nor does her baby girl. A thin shaft of light shows under the door. S. gets up and softly, without waking anyone, leans over little Britt. The baby is asleep on her back and S. sees her elongated pale face and fair hair. The little boy is asleep as well, his hair is so thick. There is no difference between them and no one could say which of the two is the child of a criminal. Both have beautifully formed ears, long fingers, little noses, mouths, even eyebrows. These two children are now beings with a separate life.

S. touches the hand of the sleeping baby boy. He closes his tiny fist around her extended finger.

The longer she looks at him, the more she begins to remember a forgotten image. His face reminds her of someone, she has seen the shape of that chin somewhere, that face, that dark hair . . . S. takes the album out of her backpack. Her photograph is on the first page. She is nine months old in the picture. She is lying on her tummy, straining to hold her head up. Perhaps because she has a big curl on top of her head. She is wearing only a top. She looks worried, as if she cannot make her mind up whether to cry or laugh. S. does not like this picture, she does not recognise herself in the plump sombre little child. In the other photograph, she is sitting in her chair on the balcony, she looks more cheerful, her hair is longer but she still has that funny lock on her head, a lock they will soon cut off.

In the next picture she is sitting on the bed. She is almost three and next to her is her sister who is only a few months old. S. looks at the photograph carefully. She carries it to the lamp. The likeness to the baby boy that she only sensed a few minutes ago is now glaring. This new-born baby has the face of her sister. S. stares at the photograph, then at his face: the pronounced cheekbones and chin which is already showing a dimple, the pouting lips, the shape of the ears, the big dark eyes, the frown . . . even their hands are similar.

S. remembers the day they were getting ready to take a stroll and her mother gave her L. to hold. The stroller was ready. S. had put on her new patent leather shoes. L. was wearing a little knitted dress. She had a white ribbon in her long dark hair. She held out her little hands and smiled at her. S. has never forgotten that smile. Now it is obvious to her that she has no way of accepting their death as fact. It is merely absence, like a void edged with ice. When they surface in her memory this way, she simply sees them. She sees them walking and talking, here, right beside her. She feels that they are warm and breathing, even if she can no longer touch them. She knows then that they exist somewhere in a parallel world, alive and dead at the same time. Just as she herself feels at times, both alive and dead.

S. cannot take her eyes off the child. What will happen to him? How many such children will be born without their fathers ever knowing about them? M. once told her that while they were raping her the soldiers had told her that she would give birth to their Serbian child and that they would force all of these Muslim women to give birth to Serbian children. Where are those soldiers now? If children are born, they will be born to these women and they, not their unknown fathers, will decide their fate. Not one of these children will know who their real father is. The mothers will disown them and give them up for adoption. Somebody else will give them a name and a country.

The children of war are in any case doomed to grow up living a lie. And should it happen that one of the mothers keeps the child, she will have to lie to it. She will have to invent for the child a father, a family, a past. Which is the greater, the right to a father or the right to the truth, S. wonders, as she leans over his cot. She senses the answer. To tell the child the truth would be to add yet another injustice to the one already done to it.

And she, what would she tell him? She would lie and say that his father had died a heroic death while trying to liberate his town. This child has the right to a father-hero. She would find it hard to invent and describe in detail this father's face, voice or habits. Hardest of all, perhaps, would be for her to think up a love story for this non-existent man.

Which story would be better for this child, the one the adoptive Swedish mother will tell him, or the one she, his mother, would tell him?

Both would lie, except only one of these stories would mean victory over the horror of war. Victory over herself, thinks S., dropping her hand down toward the child. Only his mother could show him that the hate from which his life emerged can be transformed into love. One day she will tell him that he is her child, hers alone. That he has no father—because this is the truth. His tiny body squirms. She touches his cheek and hair. As she goes back to bed she is for the first time overwhelmed by a feeling of utter tranquillity.

Again she dreams the same dream. She is walking in town, it is a big town. She sees lots of cars, bustling crowds on the streets. As if it is a holiday and people are taking a stroll and window-shopping. In the crowd she recognises the face of a man. He too is strolling from window to window, calm, relaxed, his hands in his pockets. It is summer and he is wearing light blue trousers and a white shirt. S. slowly walks over to him, she has a knife in her hand. She is prepared for this meeting, she is expecting him. She is holding the knife in her hand so that nobody will notice it. Walking rapidly she gets nearer. She has to take care not to lose him in the crowd or that he does not turn around and recognise her. That no one sees the knife in her hand as she draws it. That no one warns him. Or shouts prematurely, or stops her, thinking she is a dangerous lunatic.

She is not afraid. She listens to the rush of her own blood. She feels the flex of her own muscles. She does not hear the sounds around her. She is so focused on what she knows has got to happen now. She is close, very close: justice will now be done! She will have her revenge! She is already gripped by the sweet taste, a kind of slow intoxication with her own strength, as if the mere intention is enough.

She is almost there now. The man is standing at a window display of cameras. With her right hand she stabs him in the stomach. As always in dreams, she is surprised by how quickly and smoothly the knife slides into the tissue. He turns around and looks at her, his eyes wide open. He leans his hand against the window and slowly slides down leaving a trail of blood. She turns around, afraid that passers-by will notice that something has happened. No one seems to be paying any attention to them. He is holding his stomach now, teetering as if about to fall, but still on his feet. A dark red stain quickly spreads on his white shirt. S. starts moving away. Then she sees surprise in his eyes. She knows that the man does not recognise her. He does not remember who she is. Her revenge becomes pointless. S. stands next to him on the sidewalk and cries.

She wakes up. The sense of despair is still there, inside her, lodged in her breast, momentarily eradicating the difference between dream and consciousness. She looks at her hand and wonders whether she would really have the strength to deal such a blow. Suddenly she understands the recurrent dream and why it keeps coming back: if he has forgotten her, his victim, then she must not forget him or her own past. Their murderers need to forget, but their victims must not let them.

She sleeps peacefully for a while longer.

This happens just before daybreak. The baby is upset and starts to cry. Softly at first, then more and more loudly. S. is afraid that he will wake Maj and Britt. She picks him up to calm him. The baby keeps crying. S. unbuttons her night gown. The milk is running. She places her nipple in the baby's mouth. He sucks on it hungrily. S. feels his little body utterly relax. She draws him closer. Tears stream down her face, her neck, her breasts.

A PENGUIN READERS GUIDE TO

S.

Slavenka Drakulić

AN INTRODUCTION TO

S.

A Novel about the Balkans

"War is merely a general term, a collective noun for so many individual stories." —from S.

Humiliation of every kind—emotional and physical—abounds in Croatian journalist Slavenka Drakulić's stark, slender novel *S.* First, there is the indignity of being singled out from your neighbors, arrested for the crime of ethnic inferiority. Then there is the shame of watching the respected, older men of the community herded like cattle into a yard and shot; the pain of losing your home, clothing, money, and all personal items in a single morning; the horror of being thrown into an internment camp where a blanket on a cement floor is your bed, an open field surrounded by leering soldiers the toilet. But the cruelest injury, the one most difficult to survive, is the repeated rape and torture for the entertainment of male soldiers, oftentimes the men with whom you might have exchanged casual hellos on a village street the week before.

Such are the unfathomable sufferings of S., an urbane schoolteacher from Sarajevo who is arrested one sunny morning merely for being the child of a Muslim father and a Serbian mother. Her story may be fictional but the events are drawn from a horrifying reality—the unchecked, violent abuse of thousands of women during the Balkan war in the early 1990s. Drakulić, the author of *Café Europa* and *The Taste of a Man*, is a master at depicting the humanity of people against the backdrop of war, corruption, and social change.

In her novel *The Taste of a Man*, called by *Elle* "stunningly good . . . superbly crafted, with a journalist's eye for detail and a poet's feel for emotional truth," Drakulić examines exile, social taboos, and confession through a taut, chilling tale of obsessive love between a Polish student and a married Brazilian professor. In *Café Europa*, a collection of personal essays, Drakulić dissects post-Communist life in Eastern Europe with wit, disdain, and reflection, as she observes changing street names, Eurostyle cafes popping up on every other street corner, and a palpable yearning for all things Western. Her chief protest, though, is what she sees as an ingrained tendency in Eastern European society to disregard civic responsibility. "How does a person who is a product of a totalitarian society," she asks, "learn responsibility, individuality, initiative?" Moral duty and individual choice are issues very much at the heart of much of her writing, especially in *S.*

Before she became a novelist, Drakulić was a journalist who wrote extensively on life and war in the Balkans. Her *New York Times* op-ed piece from December, 1992 was one of the first to expose the Serbian frenzy of mass rapes of Muslim and Croatian women. With *S.*, her fourth novel, what started out as pure reportage transformed, through five years of research, into a fictionalized account of one woman who represents the thousands interred in Bosnian death camps.

In the late autumn of 1992, Drakulić set out to write a book of eyewitness accounts of rape during the Balkan war. She met and interviewed women, mostly Bosnians, Muslims, and some Croats, in refugee camps in Zagreb and Karlovac. Later, she read the testimonies of hundreds of others gathered together by the Center for War Crimes in Bosnia. "I remember the first [rape] victim I talked to," Drakulić said in an interview, "she was willing to talk—but it was impossible for her to talk about what happened to her. . . .

She could not stop shaking. It then occurred to me for the first time, her story was precisely in what she could not say. And I must find a way to say it for her."

While Drakulić would encounter many more women too traumatized to recount the horrors inflicted on them, other women opened up to her, painstakingly reciting names, dates, and places, thus beginning the long road to recovery. What S. endured—from the "women's room" to the unbearable realization that she is pregnant—is inspired by these personal accounts.

Although it is estimated that somewhere between 25,000 and 60,000 Muslim and Croatian women were raped during the Bosnian war, Drakulić knew that numbers like these, no matter how staggering, are faceless and reductive when simply quoted in news reports. "The word 'war,'" she observes, "has recently become tamed and domesticated in our vocabulary like a domestic animal, almost a pet." Likewise, "rape" is ironically minimized and depersonalized by the magnitude of the crime. With S., she puts a human face on the atrocities of the war and, through the life of one woman, provides insight into the psychology of trauma, violation, and postwar life.

As S. watches other women selected from the camp and forced into the women's room where they will be raped at the whim of Serbian soldiers, S. "cannot let go of her belief that something will save her." Of course nothing does, and it is soon her turn. There are many devastating moments in *S.*, where false hopes overshadow reality and the effects of war are visited unremittingly on the psyche of the victims. S. deludes herself, thinking maybe the stay will be brief, or the rumors of death untrue, or the young soldier who was once my neighbor will explain that I don't belong here. Ordinary women, now transformed, steal, lie, even murder, to protect themselves or their family's dignity. Drakulić illustrates the impossibility of knowing how we would act in the same situation. Survival is purely atavistic. Displacement shatters any connection to our former selves. There is no solidarity with others, just the isolated struggle to stay alive.

Hailed as "one of the strongest books about war you will ever read. . . . A work of great humanity" by *The Philadelphia Inquirer* and described as "searing, haunting, powerful and fresh" by *The San Francisco Chronicle, S.* has received international attention and acclaim. "Drakulić is a voice to be trusted in an echo chamber of lies . . . and *S.* is fiction with the terrible authority of truth" (Michael Ignatieff).

A Conversation with Slavenka Drakulić

How were you able to get these women to talk about their experiences in the camps when rape is such a taboo topic, especially among Muslims?

After the Bosnian war, a strange thing happened: many women began talking about the mass rapes, perhaps for the first time in history. They talked to reporters and health workers, to the representatives of the international community, and so forth. Several collections of their eyewitness accounts were then published. It was not easy to get them talking, especially at first. They were still in shock, distrustful, and afraid to speak out about what happened to them. The reasons for opening up were different for each victim. The obvious presence of the media in the camps brought pressure to reveal the truth about the systematic rape of these Muslim women by the Serbian army and paramilitary. Other women were convinced that they should report what happened, regardless of the consequences. They understood that there were too many victims to cover up the crimes. The women who spoke were brave, considering the patriarchal culture they come from. But these women were only able to recount the facts—the names of the men who raped them or the names of their husbands' murderers—they could not speak about their own feelings. So, in a way, I wanted to fill this void with my imagination. Therefore, the only "invented," or rather imagined, part of the novel is the description of S.'s feelings, emotions, reactions, her inner life. . . .

What has your own experience with the war been like apart from your responsibilities as a reporter? Was your family affected?

My novel deals with the war in Bosnia, not in Croatia, where I am from. Bosnia was much more devastating, it lasted four years, some 250,000 were killed, Sarajevo and Mostar destroyed. I lived in Zagreb and in comparison to Sarajevo, Zagreb was untouched by the war. So was my family. I mean, nobody was killed or wounded, no houses bombed. . . . However, in my opinion, there is nobody from over here who was not changed by this war. My family split up, my daughter left the country. There is an enormous difference between somebody losing a family member or somebody suffering psychologically. Yet, all of us were forced to go through a catharsis, to face the unexpected and unacceptable. In the war, I learned that you truly don't know yourself, there is no way to predict your own reactions. We all believe we are good, but actually we don't really know until we are put to the test. War is just such a test.

Why did you give S. just an initial as a first name? Doesn't that distance the reader from the character?

No, I don't think so. The initial has to do with her identity, her sense of her own identity. The moment soldiers walked into her village, she was deprived of it. She was reduced to her nationality, it did not matter any longer who she was, how old, what profession she had . . . she was just a Muslim—a Muslim woman. If she had been a man instead, perhaps she would have been killed immediately. And, actually, the process of depersonalization started much earlier, with "hate speech" in the media, with inciting antagonism between nationalities. . . . In the camp, S. is nobody, just a prisoner. She might as well have been identified by a number. The other reason for giving her only an initial is because it makes it more difficult for a reader to think: well, this story only concerns that particular person, it is an aberration, it cannot happen to me, to us. . . . This is wrong, no society is exempted from nationalism, xenophobia, war, rape, killings.

Based on your interviews with the survivors of rape, how widespread do you think the women's rooms were?

It seems that there were many and varied kinds of "women's rooms." That is, there were numerous brothels filled with sex slaves, there were "normal" camps where women were abused, and there were camps with a special group of women kept in such rooms for entertainment of the soldiers. Women were sometimes raped publicly when the soldiers entered a village, or in the "privacy" of their own apartments and houses. There were many ways of humiliating them.

Please explain the role of rape in the efficacy of ethnic cleansing.

What is the aim of ethnic cleansing? It is to ethnically cleanse a territory, remove the "others" in order to create a nation-state. It is difficult to kill two million people, in this case Bosnian Muslims. It requires time and means that the Serbs did not have. Therefore, you have to chase them away from a certain territory, you have to frighten them. Public humiliation is a very effective way of scaring people away. And mass rape is the most horrifying means of humiliation, not only for women but for a whole population. You shame women, you soil them. . . . Rape is about power, about one group of soldiers sending a clear message of intimidation to another group.

Have you followed the lives of any of the women you interviewed? Do you know what their situations are like now and how they are dealing with the past?

It was hard to follow the lives of women, because they became refugees in countries other than Croatia. But I know some other women whom I did not interview for this book who had similar experiences. There are those who are desperately trying to create a new life, but there are others who came back to Bosnia. The stories differ. There are a few cases where mothers kept their babies conceived in a rape, I know of two such cases. I think to deal with such a past is a life-long battle. I have a feeling that these women live very much in the past. They are lucky if they manage to live in the present at all.

The ending of S. *is quite hopeful. Is that because this a fictionalized account? Did you consider alternate endings?*

I did not consider alternate endings and I am not convinced that this ending is so hopeful. The consequences of accepting a child conceived by rape are grave. The child will have, in a way, a completely false identity and the mother will be responsible for it. It is an enormous responsibility. Really, what do you tell such a child as he or she is growing up? The truth? Imagine the child's horror. I would say that the end of the novel can be interpreted in several different ways, it is certainly not simply optimistic.

Questions for Discussion

1. The title of *S.* outside of the U.S. is *As If I Am Not There.* What happens to S. and the other prisoners as the past becomes more distant and the present more surreal?

2. The women do strange things to survive. One of the most startling is that S. finds a cosmetic bag and insists on applying full makeup before her forced rendezvous with the Captain. What is her rationale for doing this? How does it help her to survive and define who she's become?

3. S. must be on her guard with the Captain so as not to upset or anger him in any way. Yet, although she is trapped as his mistress, she says she does not hate him. Why?

4. Varlam Shalamov, himself a concentration camp survivor, is quoted on the opening page of *S.* as saying, "A human being survives by his ability to forget." Yet S. comes out of the camp plagued by something that will keep her from forgetting—she is pregnant. How does this increase S.'s isolation?

5. Drakulić explores the conflict between fear and morality for both the inmates and the soldiers. Do the inmates have a responsibility towards each other? Are they able to protect each other?

6. Drakulić writes that S.'s entire past "has spilled out of her body with this child." Is forgiveness or redemption possible through the birth of this innocent child who was created out of hate?

7. Elie Wiesel describes in his memoirs of the Holocaust the typical unwillingness of prisoners to confront reality. No one questions what is happening. How does Drakulić bring this same sense of

passivity to the characters in *S.*? Even after the villagers hear gunshots, why don't they believe that evil awaits them?

8. "But the soldiers are no longer people either, except they are less aware of it." Can one pity or begin to understand the actions of the civilians who became the soldiers in this war—the killers, murderers, and rapists?

9. How will S. cope with reality outside of the camps, a world "with its regularly flying planes and smiling flight attendants," a world that also produced the women's room?

10. Drakulić supplies virtually no personal history about S. or information about the politics of the war, focusing solely on the experiences of S.'s prison life. Does this affect our ability to relate to S.'s surreal journey from citizen to rape victim to refugee?

Guide written by Elizabeth Halpern

Other Slavenka Drakulić titles available from Penguin

THE TASTE OF A MAN

"Stunningly good . . . Superbly crafted, with a journalist's eye for detail and a poet's feel for emotional truth, the tale is so hauntingly intelligent and rationally observed it seems realer than real." —*Elle*

She is a Polish graduate student, finishing her doctorate in New York. He is a Brazilian anthropologist, in the city on a three-month research grant. They meet by chance in the New York Public Library, fall in love, and move into a tiny apartment together. In the tradition of *Damage*, *The Taste of a Man* is a breathtakingly erotic, profoundly intelligent tale of love based on pure appetite that will thrill readers with its unflinching candor, even as it shocks them with its horrifying conclusion.

ISBN 0-14-026622-4

CAFÉ EUROPA

"Insightful . . . The book not only helps to illuminate the political and social problems facing much of Eastern Europe, but also sheds light on the daily lives of its residents, their emotional habits, fears and dreams." —*The New York Times*

In the place of the fallen Berlin Wall there is a chasm between East and West, consisting of the different way people continue to live and understand the world. Little bits—or intimations—of the West are gradually making their way East: Boutiques carrying Levis and tiny food shops called "Supermarket" are multiplying on main boulevards. But even though there is a "Café Europa," complete with Viennese-style coffee and "Western" décor, in just about every Eastern European city, the acceptance of the East by the rest of Europe continues to prove much more elusive.

ISBN 0-14-027772-2

FOR THE BEST IN PAPERBACKS, LOOK FOR THE 

In every corner of the world, on every subject under the sun, Penguin represents quality and variety—the very best in publishing today.

For complete information about books available from Penguin—including Puffins, Penguin Classics, and Arkana—and how to order them, write to us at the appropriate address below. Please note that for copyright reasons the selection of books varies from country to country.

In the United Kingdom: Please write to *Dept. EP, Penguin Books Ltd, Bath Road, Harmondsworth, West Drayton, Middlesex UB7 0DA.*

In the United States: Please write to *Penguin Putnam Inc., P.O. Box 12289 Dept. B, Newark, New Jersey 07101-5289* or call 1-800-788-6262.

In Canada: Please write to *Penguin Books Canada Ltd, 10 Alcorn Avenue, Suite 300, Toronto, Ontario M4V 3B2.*

In Australia: Please write to *Penguin Books Australia Ltd, P.O. Box 257, Ringwood, Victoria 3134.*

In New Zealand: Please write to *Penguin Books (NZ) Ltd, Private Bag 102902, North Shore Mail Centre, Auckland 10.*

In India: Please write to *Penguin Books India Pvt Ltd, 11 Panchsheel Shopping Centre, Panchsheel Park, New Delhi 110 017.*

In the Netherlands: Please write to *Penguin Books Netherlands bv, Postbus 3507, NL-1001 AH Amsterdam.*

In Germany: Please write to *Penguin Books Deutschland GmbH, Metzlerstrasse 26, 60594 Frankfurt am Main.*

In Spain: Please write to *Penguin Books S. A., Bravo Murillo 19, 1° B, 28015 Madrid.*

In Italy: Please write to *Penguin Italia s.r.l., Via Benedetto Croce 2, 20094 Corsico, Milano.*

In France: Please write to *Penguin France, Le Carré Wilson, 62 rue Benjamin Baillaud, 31500 Toulouse.*

In Japan: Please write to *Penguin Books Japan Ltd, Kaneko Building, 2-3-25 Koraku, Bunkyo-Ku, Tokyo 112.*

In South Africa: Please write to *Penguin Books South Africa (Pty) Ltd, Private Bag X14, Parkview, 2122 Johannesburg.*